ROOM OF SHADOWS

ROOM OF SHADOWS

RONALD KIDD

ALBERT WHITMAN & COMPANY
CHICAGO, ILLINOIS

Other books by

RONALD KIDD

Night on Fire
Dreambender

Library of Congress Cataloging-in-Publication
data is on file with the publisher.

Text copyright © 2017 by Ronald Kidd
Cover illustration © 2017 by Rachel Cloyne
Published in 2017 by Albert Whitman & Company
ISBN 978-0-8075-6805-7

Printed in the United States of America
10 9 8 7 6 5 4 3 2 1 BP 22 21 20 19 18 17

Design by Jordan Kost

For more information about Albert Whitman & Company,
visit our website at www.albertwhitman.com.

To Russ, Carol, Bill, and family
and always
to Yvonne and Maggie

"Ghastly grim and ancient Raven
	wandering from the Nightly shore—
Tell me what thy lordly name is
	on the Night's Plutonian shore!"
		Quoth the Raven, "Nevermore."
—Edgar Allan Poe, "The Raven"

Contents

I would have killed him, but I had no hands.

I had no feet. No head. No body. Just a spirit floating in the darkness—helpless, filled with rage.

He betrayed me. He destroyed my plan. The plan was beautiful. You would have laughed at how clever it was.

Death—defeated! Life—regained!

And the best part? A story in the bargain. The darkest, foulest, most magnificent story ever written: "A Journey to Death and Back."

Hah! Read the words. Tremble at the thought.

I tell you, death is a way station, a curtain, a veil. Pierce the veil! Come with me to a room of shadows. Horror going. Triumph in return.

That was my plan, and he destroyed it.

I will get him someday. I will get them all.

Chapter 1
A Dragon

It was the year I discovered anger.

I thought I knew all about it. Everyone gets mad, right? You stub your toe or burn your finger. You yell. Maybe you hit something. It flashes through you like lightning, then it's gone.

If that's your idea of anger, congratulations. You're one of the lucky ones.

I'm talking about a different kind of anger. This kind moves in on you. It takes root in the basement—pulsing, growing, the color of a bruise. You don't even know it's there. Then one day the floor heaves and it bursts out, pinning you to the wall, overwhelming you. And there's nothing you can do.

For me, that day came last fall. My mom and I had moved from our neighborhood outside Baltimore to an old house downtown. We didn't want to move, but my dad had had other ideas, most of them involving a woman named Gretchen, someone he worked with. Gretchen moved to New York, and so did he. Just like that. Don't get me started.

So, what do you do when you find out you'll be living on just one salary? You pack up your stuff. You say good-bye to your friends. You get in the car and drive off. You don't look back.

We moved downtown to be near my mom's work. She's a librarian at the Enoch Pratt Free Library, which is a fancy name for the Baltimore public library. She threw herself into her job. I threw myself into a new school, the way you might wad up a sheet of paper and toss it into the trash. Eighth grade with a bunch of strangers. New people to meet. New things to learn. Wake me when it's over.

The school was actually two schools. Marshall High was a big old brick building across from a row of businesses and deserted factories. Next door was my school, Marshall Middle, an even older building. Besides the name, we shared a football team, a mascot, and a band that my mom had made me join, saying it would be a good way to meet people. Even in the band, though, I mostly kept to myself. I figured I could make friends later if I felt like it.

I mostly just wandered from class to class, a short, skinny, thirteen-year-old kid with dark hair and bright eyes. If you talked to me, I might nod, or maybe I'd just keep moving.

My mom and I lived close to school, so I would walk home. That day she had asked me to stop by

Lexington Market to pick up something for dinner. It was this famous old market with hundreds of stalls that had every kind of food you could imagine. Of course, my mom knew that if I was picking, there was just one choice: crab cakes from Faidley's, Baltimore's finest.

I bought the crab cakes, picked out a candy bar, and was heading home when I heard a voice.

"Hey, David!"

I turned around. It was Jake Bragg, a kid who had appointed himself mayor of eighth grade. Jake and his buddies hung around outside campus, smoking and telling stories about their latest exploits with bad cops and bad girls, stories that took place in an imaginary land where they weren't idiots. Jake had introduced himself to me on my first day of school, saying he would check in later to see how I was doing. I guess later had arrived.

I watched as he strolled up to me. He was a big, dark-haired kid with eyes that never blinked. I'm not kidding. His eyeballs must have been like sandpaper.

"What've you got?" he asked, nodding toward my shopping bag.

I shrugged. "Dinner."

"Can I see?"

I should have said no. I should have told him to take his dry, scratchy eyeballs and go bother someone else. But I didn't. I opened the bag.

At my old school, I once built a science project to demonstrate cause and effect. It was a crazy contraption with slides, traps, levers, doors, and pinwheels, connected by yards and yards of plastic tubing I had sawed in half lengthwise to form a chute. At the science fair, I set a rubber ball at the top and gave it a push. You wouldn't believe what happened. Things dropped, turned, opened, closed, cranked, and slid, until at the very bottom, a wooden stick poked out and turned over a cup of water. The water soaked a little squiggly green sponge. The sponge grew and grew, and before you knew it, you were staring at a dragon.

That's the way it was when I opened the bag. That one little push set everything in motion. Wheels turned, gears cranked, doors opened. At the bottom, waiting, was the sponge.

Who would have thought it really was a dragon?

Jake looked into the bag. "Are those crab cakes?"

"Yeah, why?"

"I love crab cakes."

I felt something stir, way down deep. "So?"

"You know," said Jake, "that school we go to, it's dangerous. You're new. I wouldn't expect you to know. Some pretty rough kids go there."

"Thanks for the information," I said.

"They'll beat you up. I've watched them do it. When someone new comes along, they jump him. I hate to see it. Of course, it doesn't have to be that way."

He took a step toward me. I could hear him breathe. Usually I would have been scared.

I'm not big or tough. At school, when other

guys were wrestling on the playground, I was the one sitting on a bench, reading. Maybe Jake had spotted me there. Maybe he figured I'd be an easy target.

He said, "If they try to bother you, I could take care of them."

"What do you mean?"

"Protection," he said. "I'll make sure you're safe."

He gave me a cold, hard stare.

Go ahead, blink, I thought. Just once.

"The thing is," Jake said, "there's a price."

"What's the price?" I asked.

"Let's start with those crab cakes."

He reached into the bag. A hand shot out and grabbed his wrist. I was surprised to see that it was mine.

I heard myself say, "Don't do that."

He looked up, amazed. "You touched me. Nobody touches me."

After ripping his hand free, he snatched the bag and gave me a shove. I staggered back, tripped over the curb, and fell down. As I watched, he scooped out a handful of crab cake—my dinner—and shoved it into his mouth, grinning.

The floor heaved. Something big and dark came out. I think it had been in there a long time—before school, before we moved, ever since my dad left. It had started small and had grown day by day. Now it was huge. It came bursting out, and I couldn't stop it.

I got to my feet and strode toward him.

"These crab cakes are good," he said.

I punched him in the mouth, right where the crab cake had been.

"Hey!" he said in a muffled voice.

He dropped the bag and swung at me. I hit him in the nose, hard. There was a crunching sound. Blood spurted out.

I hit him again. "Blink," I said.

"Huh?"

"Blink."

He blinked. I punched him in the stomach. He

doubled over, and I brought my fists down on the back of his head.

It felt like a dream, the kind where you can do anything—walk through walls, climb buildings, destroy things just by looking at them.

He fell to the ground, moaning. I kicked him in the ribs. I kicked him again and again.

I kicked him for the way my dad had left us. I kicked him for the friends I had lost. I kicked him for the new teachers who hadn't learned my name and for all the people I'd met who thought quiet meant stupid and small meant weak.

I was surprised to find that it felt good. The more I did it, the better it felt.

Jake kept moaning. He had closed his eyes, and his face was bloody.

I started to kick him again, when someone grabbed me from behind. A voice said, "Oh my God."

I looked over my shoulder and saw a taxi driver. He had pulled over, jumped out of his cab, and wrapped his arms around my chest.

The man stared at Jake. "What have you done?"

"He took my crab cakes," I said.

Chapter 2
Cloaked in Shadow

A crowd had gathered, and they glanced uneasily at the person who looked like me. They were horrified, and so was I. Who was he? Where had he come from? What would he do next?

There were sirens. An ambulance pulled up to the curb, and they loaded Jake Bragg inside. A police officer appeared next to me. He took my arm and led me away.

I learned about the back seat of a squad car and

the inside of a police station. They had a smell. I
think it was fear. I spent a lot of time sitting and
waiting. My mind raced. I pictured myself in jail,
eating scraps of food from a tray they pushed under the door.

Years passed, or maybe it was hours. Finally
one of the police sergeants, a big man with dark
skin and kind eyes, came in and sat down beside
me. Above his uniform pocket was a nameplate:
Clark.

"You're a lucky boy," said Sergeant Clark. "The
hospital called. That kid you beat up, he has a con-
cussion, but it looks like he'll be okay."

"That's great," I said.

"We checked up on you. You've never been in
trouble. What happened out there?"

I didn't know what to say. "I guess I lost my
temper."

"The police have a boxing club for kids, and
I'm in charge. Maybe you should join."

"This might sound funny," I said, "but I don't

like violence."

He cocked his head and gazed at me. "You're different."

You have no idea, I thought.

He said, "We're going to give you a break. You're free to go."

I stared at him. "I am?"

"Don't let it happen again. Right?"

I remembered the feeling when my fist smashed Jake's nose. It was something like joy.

I shivered. "Right."

"Your mother's here. She'll take you home."

Sergeant Clark thought he was letting me off easy. He had never met my mom. I looked up and saw her in the waiting area, pacing back and forth. She was tall, with long red hair and freckles. When she was mad, the freckles blended together. Today there was just one big freckle.

* * *

"You what!"

We were sitting in our car, parked behind the

police station.

"Mom, stop saying that. They told you what happened. I tried to explain."

"I'm a librarian. This doesn't happen to librarians." She grabbed my shoulders and swung me around to face her. "We are civilized people. We don't fight. Do you understand?"

"He threatened me," I told her.

"They said he was on the ground, bleeding, and you were kicking him."

I looked away.

She said, "What in God's name were you doing?"

"I don't know."

"You don't know? You almost killed someone!"

"That's not true."

She jerked my head back to look at her. Her gaze cut me like a knife. "This is serious. Don't you see? You could have ruined your life."

Her voice broke. Her shoulders slumped, and she let go of me.

"Look, David," she said, "I know it's been rough. Your father runs off, we move, you change schools. But this…"

She shook her head.

"I'm sorry," I said.

"That's not good enough."

She wiped her eyes, then started the car. As she drove, I could see her thinking. Finally she said, "I'm grounding you."

"Mom…"

"You'll go straight home after school every day and stay there."

"For how long?" I asked.

"As long as it takes. Until you learn to control your anger." She glanced at me, her knuckles white on the steering wheel. "And so help me, if I hear about you fighting again, you'll never get out."

"Can I—"

"Shut up, David. Just shut up."

A few minutes later we pulled up to a curb. I got out of the car, in front of the place where I'd be spending my days and nights.

It was a house. We were living there. But it didn't feel like home. Home was where we used to live, in a neighborhood, with trees, lawns, and friends. This place was different—very different. My mom said they gave us a break on the rent, and I could see why.

The house stood tall and gray on a hillside, like a boulder, like a dark cloud. It had two floors plus an attic and narrow windows like eyes. The paint was peeling. There were loose shingles on the roof, and on top was a weather vane that turned even when there seemed to be no wind. Stone steps led to a thick wooden door. Gables bent across the door and over an attic window. There was a porch, but it wasn't the kind where your aunt Bessie would sit and swing.

It disappeared around the side of the house, cloaked in shadow, so you could never quite make out what was there.

Across the front of the yard was a rusted

metal fence. Behind it, an old oak tree spread its branches like a spiderweb over the house. One of the branches reached the second-floor window of my bedroom. Since moving I'd had trouble sleeping, and sometimes late at night I would climb out and use the tree to escape the place. I wouldn't do much—just sit under the tree or walk around the block—but it made me feel better, like I was in control.

When the landlord had shown us the house, he had called it a Victorian. He'd said it dated back to the late 1800s, when it had been built on the ruins of an earlier residence. Over the years, the homes around it had been torn down and replaced by stores and other businesses, many with apartments above them. Some of the stores had been boarded up. Others were still operating. But the house lingered on.

I stared up at it. It stared back.

"Get used to it," said my mom. "For the next few weeks, this is your world."

I opened the metal gate. My mom walked inside, and I followed. The gate clanged shut behind me like the door of a jail cell.

Chapter 3
My Pet Bat

I had seen her a few times at school. She was short with black hair and brown eyes. She was always smiling, and I could never figure out why.

A few days after the fight, I ran into her—literally. Heading off to school one morning, I had just come out of the gate and was looking back over my shoulder at the house. As I walked, I bumped into someone.

"Hey!" she said.

Turning around, I found myself facing her. She wore faded jeans and a T-shirt, and her hair was pulled back in a ponytail. A pile of textbooks lay at her feet.

"Sorry," I mumbled. I squatted down and gathered up her books.

"That's okay," she said. "I was looking at it too. You know, the house."

"You were?"

"Someone actually lives there. Can you believe it?"

I got to my feet and handed her the books.

"Thanks," she said. She tucked them under one arm and extended her hand. "I'm Libby Morales."

Her hand was soft and warm. "I'm David Cray," I said.

I nodded toward her books. "You should get a backpack."

"I have one. It's in the shop."

"The shop?"

"My dad's a fix-it man. He repairs everything.

There's just one catch—the paying customers come first. My mom has appliances sitting on his shelf that are older than I am."

She glanced down the street. "I should get to school. Are you going?"

"Huh? Oh, yeah."

"Then come on."

We walked together, past liquor stores and pawnshops. Libby did most of the talking, which was fine with me. It gave me a chance to look at her. I knew she was in the eighth grade, the same as me, but she looked older, especially around the eyes. She had a way of nodding as she spoke, kind of a built-in yes. When she smiled, her face glowed like the sun.

It turned out she lived down the street from our house, in an apartment over her father's shop, with her brother, sister, and parents. I hadn't thought of our block as a neighborhood, but she was a neighbor.

As we rounded the corner toward school, she

glanced at me. "So, it's not true after all."

"What do you mean?"

"You're not eight feet tall. You don't have horns or torture kittens."

I must have looked puzzled.

"Look, David, I haven't been honest with you," she said. "I knew who you were as soon as I heard your name. Everybody at school knows. You're the boy who beat up Jake Bragg."

Suddenly it seemed important to explain. "He threatened me. He wanted me to pay him for protection. I never beat up anybody before."

She studied my face. "Really?"

"What are they saying about me?"

"Let's put it this way," she said. "I don't think you need protection, from Jake Bragg or anybody else."

Great. I'd barely started at school, and everybody was afraid of me. Well, almost everybody.

Libby smiled. "If you don't torture kittens, what do you do?"

"Not much," I said. "I'm grounded."

"Because of the fight?"

I nodded. "It's okay. There's hope. I'll be out when I'm forty-three."

"Ouch."

"Go to school, come home. Go to school, come home. Nice, huh?"

She said, "You must be tired of your apartment."

I didn't want to lie to her. It didn't seem right.

"Libby," I said, "I haven't been honest with you either. You know that house we were looking at? The creepy one with broken shutters? Someone does live there. It's my mom and me."

She stopped and stared at me.

I shrugged. "Well, there's also my pet bat."

She giggled, and the giggle turned into a laugh. Relieved, I laughed along with her.

"David Cray," she said, "you are full of surprises."

"Is that good?"

"I like surprises," she said.

I am Poe. I wrote stories, but none so glorious and appalling as the story I will tell you now, the one that seized me and would not let go.

The story began, as it ended, with death.

Virginia, my beloved wife, died. Without Ginny my light was gone, my soul split. The only thing left was words. Oh, tender, harsh, empty words!

I planned a magazine, called the Stylus. *I sailed to Richmond to raise money and left two months later, a fat roll of bills in my pocket. All was well, or so I thought.*

On the way back, my head began to throb as if caught in a vise. I staggered off the ship in Baltimore, where Ginny and I had spent our happiest years.

Pain! Spasms! Seizures!

I stumbled into an opium den, but the relief didn't last. I needed something stronger, and I wondered where I could get it.

A name skittered like a cockroach across my mind. Curse the day I heard it. Blast the day I remembered it. Reynolds.

Chapter 4
A Minute Before Midnight

There was something odd about the house. Sure, it was old and battered and a little off-kilter, but that's not what I mean. I'm talking about the floor plan. It wasn't right.

When I finished my homework each day, I got into the habit of exploring the house. You wouldn't believe the stuff I found—old shoes, postcards from the 1800s, antique buttons and jars. They were stuffed into nooks and crannies all over the house.

In fact, I became sort of an expert on nooks and crannies. I got to where I could spot them from down the hall or across a room—little places where you could hide things. In that house, it was like they were built in on purpose. Maybe the architect liked puzzles and games. Maybe he had a sense of humor and was laughing in his grave.

As I explored, though, I started to get the feeling that one of the nooks—or was it a cranny?—wasn't little at all. There was something strange about the floor plan. The layout of the first floor seemed normal enough, with the kitchen, my mom's bedroom, and the living room, which in the old days they called a parlor. The second floor was another matter. There was my room, a hallway, and an extra bedroom where we piled boxes and junk. But it seemed like there should be more. The rooms didn't add up. As my wise-guy teacher Mr. Sturgeon had said about my science quiz one day, the whole was greater than the sum of its parts.

There was also the strange fact that the house had a chimney, but I'd never seen a fireplace.

Curious, I found a tape measure and used it to figure out the size of the rooms. I got some paper and drew up a rough floor plan, showing the location of the walls and the places in between. Sure enough, in the middle of the floor plan, right behind my room, was a big blank space.

I went into my room and studied the back wall. What was on the other side? I put my ear to the wall, between movie posters for *The Shining* and *Invasion of the Body Snatchers*, but I didn't hear anything. I tapped the wall. It sounded hollow.

My room had a closet at the back. I got a flashlight, pulled aside the clothes hanging there, and inspected the walls. They seemed normal enough. I was about to turn away and leave when I noticed a crack near the bottom of the rear wall. It was so thin you could barely see it. I got down on my knees and, adjusting the flashlight beam, focused it on the wall. From above, the crack had been almost invisible, but down low, from a few inches away, I could see it clearly.

I wedged my fingernails into the crack and wiggled. Something shifted. I dug my nails in farther, then lifted and pushed. There was a creaking sound, and a wall panel swung outward, as if attached to very old hinges. Behind the panel was a door—an old, old door.

I shone the light on it. The wood was pitted, and the handle, lock, and other hardware were brown and tarnished. I tried the handle. It turned, but the door seemed stuck. I tried again, with no luck, then threw my shoulder against it. The door flew open, and I went stumbling inside.

I had dropped the flashlight, so I picked it up and shone it around. I was in a room about the size of mine. There was a high ceiling covered with spiderwebs, like mold on a slice of spoiled bread.

Something scuttled across the floor, taking cover behind a big, bulky object in the middle of the room. The object turned out to be a large, antique writing desk, covered with a blanket of dust and an assortment of odd items—a kerosene lantern, an old-fashioned quill pen, a sheaf of paper.

On the other side of the desk was a long, low table covered by a cloth, with a giant bird crouched on top. For a moment I thought the bird was real. Then, advancing slowly and shining my beam on it, I realized it was a carving. I blew off the dust. Mistake. A cloud rose up, thick as fog. I coughed and fired off a round of sneezes. When the dust settled, I examined the carving. It was a raven. Someone had shaped it in perfect detail, then painted coal-black feathers and eyes the color of blood. On the base were the letters *E. P.*

"Is that your name?" I asked. The raven didn't answer.

I circled the desk, and the red eyes followed me. Beside the desk, against a wall, was a grandfather clock taller than I was. The pendulum hung motionless, and the hands had stopped at one minute to twelve.

On the opposite wall was the missing fireplace. It had been bricked over. Next to it was a rectangular shape that once had been a window, and it was bricked over too. The room, for whatever reason, had been sealed. The only entrance was the secret one through my closet.

There was another object nearby, and I realized it was an old desk chair. I rolled it over to the desk and wiped off the seat with my shirtsleeve, being careful not to create another dust cloud. Then, propping up the flashlight to illuminate the area, I sat down.

You'd think the chair would have been rickety and uncomfortable, but it felt good. Leaning forward, I checked the desk drawers. In the top drawer was an ancient key.

Remembering the lock on the door, I went over and tried it. The key fit. By jiggling it, I was able to lock the door and unlock it again.

I returned to the chair, put the key back, and

checked the other drawers. They were filled with paper, blank and yellowed with age. I picked up the quill pen from the desktop. As I did, a blast of energy raced up my arm and through my body. My ears tingled, and I swear that my hair stood on end. My hand twitched, eager to do something. I went into my room and got a bottle of ink that I'd used on a calligraphy art project I'd done at school. Then I came back, took some of the yellowed paper from a drawer, and began to write.

Wild, fevered scenes leaped to mind. I was on a ship in a storm, being sucked into a huge whirling vortex. I sneaked through a dark alley, and a hairy beast jumped me from behind. I was in a hot-air balloon, floating up to the moon. Each scene was a story—eerie, thrilling, fully formed. It seemed as if the stories had already been written, but somehow I had to write them again.

As fast as the scenes came to me, I captured them on paper. My hand flashed across the pages, spewing words. When one page was filled, I tossed it to the floor and picked up another.

My shadow, hunched over and huge, flickered on the wall behind me.

I don't know how long I went on like that. It could have been an hour, maybe two. When I looked up, pages covered the floor. I was sweating. The surge of energy had passed, replaced by a low hum, like an electric current.

I glanced up at the grandfather clock. It might be daytime outside, but in this room, sealed off from the world, the time was always a minute before midnight.

I set down the pen and picked up my flashlight. I stumbled across the room and out the door, shutting it behind me and closing the wall panel.

I wasn't sure what had happened, but I knew one thing. I would be back.

Chapter 5
Surrounded by Gravestones

"Are you okay?"

We were at breakfast, and my mom was looking at me over the morning paper. Around our house, breakfast was one of the last vestiges of family life. Eating at least one meal a day together was something that years ago my dad had insisted on. After he left, my mom had started the tradition again. I guess it was her feeble attempt to hold the family together, at least what was left of it. It wasn't as if we said much, though. She would read the paper, and I would play with my phone. Heartwarming, isn't it?

"I'm fine," I mumbled.

"I don't get it," she said. "You're always tired, but all you do is go to school and come home. That is all you do, isn't it?"

"Sorry to tell you this, Mom, but I've been sneaking out to run triathlons."

"You're a wise guy," she said. "A tired wise guy."

The funny thing is, she was right. I was tired, and all I'd been doing was going to school and coming home. Of course, there was more to home than met the eye.

I had returned to the secret room, as I knew I would. Needing a better light source, I had filled the lantern with kerosene and lit it. The light was good, but as smoke curled up from the lantern, I realized it might be dangerous in a sealed room. So, on my way home from school, I stopped by the hardware store and bought an electric lantern. It operated on batteries, because I had noticed that the room had no electrical outlets. What kind of room doesn't have electrical outlets?

The visions continued to flow, from my mind to the page, from the page to the floor. Comets battered the Earth, destroying cities and towns. A plague struck, and people died off like flies. Robots sprang to life, helping humanity but plotting in secret. After days of scribbling, the paper started to pile up, forming a barrier like a wall. I liked that. It made me feel safe.

Then one day after school, it all changed.

I was sitting at the desk, writing. That day it was about people who had been buried alive. They screamed and scratched and pounded on their coffins, but no one came. The words poured out, and I tried to keep up.

There was a noise. I looked up, startled. Libby was standing there.

"Okay, don't be mad," she said.

I stared, surrounded by gravestones.

She spoke quickly, tripping over the words. "I knocked on the front door, but no one answered. I knew you were home because—well, you're always home. I figured you didn't hear me, so I pushed open the door and called your name. No answer. I started getting worried. Maybe it's the house—this place is creepy. You were here all alone. What if you got sick, or fell and hurt yourself? Maybe you were injured and bleeding. I had to find you. I looked around and noticed a light coming from your closet. I shouldn't have come in, I know. But I was scared."

She looked around the room. "What is this place? What are you doing?"

"I'm not sure," I said.

She moved to the desk and looked down at the paper I'd been scribbling on, then at the pages piled on the floor. I realized it must have seemed strange.

"I've been writing," I explained.

"I guess so."

"This story is about people trapped inside coffins."

She gave me a long, hard look. I could tell she was right on the edge—accept me and find out more, or turn away and never come back. It would have been so easy for her to leave and join the other kids at school, the ones who stared and pointed but never talked to me. I don't know why, but she stayed.

"Okay, David," she said, "this is seriously weird. You live in a haunted house. There's a secret room with no windows. And you're writing about...coffins?"

In the week since I'd discovered the room, it had become the most important thing in my life— sometimes, it seemed, the only thing—and yet I hadn't told anyone about it. Maybe I never would have if it hadn't been for Libby. With her there, it all poured out.

I told her about the floor plan and the tape measure and the big blank space. I described the hidden door and the dark room behind it. Picking up the electric lantern, I showed her the fireplace and window that had been bricked over, the carved raven, the grandfather clock with hands that never moved.

I went back to the desk, threading my way among the old, yellowed papers. They were everywhere, covered with words I barely recognized. How could I explain them?

"The stories are about coffins and beasts and monsters," I said, "but to be honest, I'm not sure who the writer is."

I described the scenes that played out in my mind and how I tried to capture them on paper. It wasn't exactly writing. It was more like taking dictation.

Glancing around the room, Libby shivered. "David, what's going on?"

Chapter 6
Snakes and Scorpions and One-Eyed Dogs

That night I had trouble sleeping. I tossed and turned, thinking about Libby and everything that had happened. She hadn't stayed long, but she had promised to come back. Part of me was glad she had shown up. Part of me was angry and wasn't sure why. Finally, tangled in the sheets, I fell asleep.

I was standing on the sidewalk, looking up at the house. As I watched, the shutters opened and seemed to blink. The house leaned toward me. An awful smell rose up, like meat that had been left in the sun. Worms wriggled out of the windows. They were headed straight for me.

I edged back, but they kept coming. There were snakes and scorpions and one-eyed dogs, snarling, slithering. I yelled, but no sound came out. So I ran, down the streets and through the gutters. A hot wind blew. The ground shook.

As I stumbled along, I heard a terrible clattering noise. I looked back, and there, spilling out of the house, came an army of skeletons. They staggered and lunged, their lipless skulls grinning. They wanted me. They hungered for me.

The clattering grew louder. The wind howled. It tugged at me like some evil vacuum cleaner, pulling me back toward the house. I grabbed a tree trunk and hung on for a moment, my body parallel to the ground, feet flapping like flags. Then I was sucked in, past the skeletons, over the snakes, through the door; dragged up the stairs, across my bedroom, and into the closet.

The wind stopped, dumping me onto the floor. Looking up, I faced a wall. My life was full of walls. Keep out. You don't belong.

Suddenly I wanted to go into the room. I needed to. Something was happening. I didn't know what, but I had to be there.

I swung back the panel, opened the door, and stepped inside. The room was the color of blood. When my eyes adjusted, I saw why. The eyes of the carved raven glowed bright red.

I moved past the raven and toward the clock, stopping in front of it. The pendulum hung motionless. Opening the case, I swung the pendulum, and the clock started tick, tick, ticking.

A moment later, the minute hand clicked to twelve. There was an awful grinding noise, and the chimes began. Low and deep, they rang through the room. My heart raced. My fists clenched. The chimes felt like blows, like what I had done to Jake Bragg.

Behind me, beneath the chimes, I heard a bumping sound, then another. Turning around, I saw the raven, its eyes glowing like lasers. There was another bump, and the carving rocked back and forth. The sounds were coming from the long, low table where the raven sat.

I edged toward the table and picked up the raven, which was warm to the touch, and moved it to the desk. The table, covered by a dingy cloth, bumped and shook. Fear gripped me, but my curiosity was stronger. Taking a deep breath, I reached out, grasped one edge of the cloth, and slowly pulled it aside.

I was amazed to see that the object beneath wasn't a table at all. It was an ancient wooden chest, carved on the sides with strange shapes and designs. As I watched, the chest seemed to vibrate, and there was a loud rattling.

I could just leave. I could blink, snap my fingers, and find myself back in bed. But then my questions would never be answered. Why was there a chest in the room? What was inside? What did it all mean?

While the clock chimed on, I reached for the chest. The lid was stuck. Gripping it with both hands, I yanked upward. The lid flew open. I stumbled and fell. Crawling forward, I reached the chest and peered inside.

I saw a body. It had stringy black hair, sunken eyes, and a mustache. As I stared, the clock chimed twelve. The eyes popped open and bore into me. The cracked lips grinned.

The body lurched to a sitting position. The arms reached for me.

I ran, bumping against the chest, tripping over my feet, staggering to the doorway. The next thing I knew, I was back in bed, wrapped in the sheets, sweating.

"David?"

I looked up and saw my mom. She sat on the edge of the bed and put her hand on my shoulder.

"You were yelling," she said. "Are you all right?"

Remembering the body, I shivered. "Bad dream," I mumbled. "I'm fine."

She leaned over and kissed me, then pulled her robe around her and left.

I stared into the darkness. Those eyes stared back at me. They wouldn't go away.

I knew what I had to do. I got out of bed and walked to the closet. Opening the panel and the door, I went inside and switched on the lantern.

The raven was on the table, and the cloth was back in place. Papers were scattered around. The clock was silent, showing a minute before twelve. The room was just as I had left it that afternoon.

To make sure, I set down the lantern, moved the raven to the desk, and pulled aside the cloth. Just as in the dream, the object beneath wasn't a table at all. It was a chest. I reached out, my hand trembling, and opened the lid.

The chest was empty.

I wanted to think it had always been empty. But maybe, part of me whispered, the dream had been real. Maybe the body had sprung out of the chest and into the world. Maybe it was lurking, grinning, watching me at that very moment.

I folded the cloth and set it aside, then shut the chest, put the raven back on top, and picked up the lantern. I checked the room one more time, then went back to bed.

I didn't sleep very well that night.

Reynolds's face was like two faces.

One side was smooth and calm. The other side, red as blood, buckled and heaved, as if boiling from the inside. When he smiled, as he was smiling now, I shuddered. Can a face rip apart?

Words oozed out. "Ah, back again."

Behind that hideous grin was knowledge I needed. Reynolds was a mesmerist, a disciple of Franz Mesmer. Mesmer believed that people have spirits, and objects do too. The spirits can reach out across the void and connect with each other. Mesmer learned to shape these spirits, to train them by putting patients into a hypnotic trance to call up memories or block out pain.

I had first met Reynolds when researching some of my stories, and I had used his ideas as the basis for several of them. Now my need was more urgent:

"Please, for the love of God, stop the pain! Keep my head from exploding!"

He induced the trance. The vise loosened. Blessed relief! Then, like a clap of thunder, it tightened again.

I opened my eyes. He shook his head sadly. "You are beyond my help."

Oh, wretched words! Oh, miserable life!

Fumbling in my pocket, I paid him a few dollars. As I did, he eyed my roll of bills greedily.

Who would have imagined it? That glimpse consigned me to hell.

Chapter 7
An Icy Breeze

It was early in the morning a few days later, and the shop was open. A neat sign hung over the door.

Second Chance

Repair and Restoration

Stepping inside, I saw a big, swarthy man who wore a leather apron and stood at a workbench. He had put a broken chair leg in a vise and was gluing it back together.

The man looked up and smiled. "I wish people

were this easy to fix," he said. "A little glue and paint—they'd be as good as new."

I thought of my dad. "What if you don't want to fix them? Maybe you just throw them away."

The man studied my face, then gestured across the room at a floor lamp with a shade made of brightly colored glass. "See that lamp? I found it at the city dump. It needed work, but now it's my favorite thing in the shop."

I heard footsteps on the stairs behind him, and Libby appeared. I noticed she was wearing her backpack.

"Hey, it's fixed," I said.

"It all gets fixed—eventually. Right, Dad?"

Chuckling, he brushed off her backpack and tightened one of the straps.

She said, "I see you've met David."

"Is that who he is? I thought he was just hanging around, looking for advice." The man wiped his hand on the apron and held it out to me. "I'm Libby's dad, Hector Morales."

"David Cray," I said. "I'm a friend of Libby's." Shaking his hand, I was impressed by the strength of his grip.

He looked back and forth from Libby to me then nodded. "Off to school, huh?"

"We could stay and help you do repairs," she told him.

"You've got better things to do," he told her. "Like, be a doctor or lawyer."

"Dad, I'm in the eighth grade."

"Not for long," he said.

She gave him a peck on the cheek, and we headed off. It was a misty morning, the way it sometimes gets in the fall. A bank of fog had rolled in from the ocean, blocking out the sun.

The shadows reminded me of the dream I'd had a few days before, and suddenly I wanted to tell Libby. I described the snakes and scorpions, the chimes, the chest, and the man inside.

"What do you think it means?" I asked.

"It means you've got a vivid imagination."

Just then the sun broke through, and she smiled. Maybe the dream wasn't so scary after all.

We didn't say anything for a while. We didn't have to. It was one of the things I was learning about Libby. When you were with her, you could just be yourself. You didn't need to fill up the spaces.

We strolled down the street, past shops that sold antiques, used books, and second-hand clothing. There was a plumbing supply store and a brickyard. People wandered by, and a few stopped at the gas station, where you could buy coffee, doughnuts, and sandwiches. Some waited at a bus stop. Cars passed by, then a bus rumbled up to the curb. A woman got off, holding her daughter's hand. She greeted a man who was sitting on the bench, and he tipped his hat. Maybe the place really was a neighborhood.

As we walked another block or two, a feeling swept over me like an icy breeze. I was sure someone was watching us. I turned and looked, but no one was there.

"Did you see anyone?" I asked Libby.

"Who?"

"I don't know."

She gave me a funny look, and we kept going.

On the next block, I glanced in a store window and saw something reflected. It was dark, like a shadow. I whirled around, but nothing was there.

"Is something wrong?" asked Libby.

I said, "Did you ever have the feeling you were being watched?"

"Look, David," she said, "don't get carried away. This is real life, not a dream."

"I thought I saw something."

She said, "I see something. You're losing it."

We turned a corner, and school loomed ahead of us. People say Marshall Middle School is a historic building, but if you ask me, it's just old. The windows are dirty, and the bricks have been blackened by years of smoke and grime. The steps leading up to the front door are cracked, with weeds poking through.

As we climbed the steps, someone shoved me from behind. I skidded to the ground, ripping my jeans and scraping my knee.

Looking up, I saw Wesley Gault, Jake Bragg's buddy. He was a skinny little kid who had earned the nickname Weasel. The odd thing was, that morning he seemed to be scared, as if he had had to build up his nerve to push me.

"Go ahead, hit me," he said, his voice shaking, "like you hit Jake."

I remembered the way Jake Bragg had grinned as he reached for my crab cakes. He had tripped something inside me. Now I felt it stirring again. I pushed it down and shook my head.

"Sorry, not today," I said.

"What's wrong? You afraid?"

"Maybe you're just too tough for me, Wesley."

I turned away, and he shoved me again. I lost my balance and landed heavily on the steps.

Wesley stood over me. A couple of his friends were behind him.

Libby knelt beside me. "David, are you okay?"

I waved her off and peered up at Wesley. Suddenly I was back at Lexington Market, beating up Jake. My face was hot. My fists were pumping. Each time they hit him, I felt stronger.

"How did you like the police station?" asked Wesley.

"Get out of here," I told him. "Go away."

"I hear it's nasty."

He glanced at his friends, and the grin crept back. "The cops want you back, David. They're saving a place for you. All you have to do is hit me."

It would be so easy to reach out, pull his legs from under him, and bash his head against the steps. I could rip away his grin. I could hurt his friends.

I closed my eyes, fighting the feeling. When I opened them, a crowd had gathered. They whispered and pointed. I felt like some kind of freak, an animal in a cage.

That's the kid who beat up Jake Bragg.

I hear he almost killed him.

Funny, he's not that big.

I could teach them a lesson. It's not what you look like. It's what you feel. It's what you see. It's the pictures that crowd into your mind and push out everything else. It's the people you'd like to hurt. It's what you can do with your bare hands.

"Watch this," Wesley told his friends.

He kicked me.

I wanted to hit him, hard. It would feel so good.

He kicked me again. His friends laughed. The crowd gathered closer.

"David!"

The voice was behind me. I turned and saw Libby. I had forgotten she was there.

"We have to go," she said.

Wesley grinned and asked me, "Is that your girlfriend?"

Libby stared at him. "What if I am?"

"Your boy's not so tough after all," said Wesley. "In fact, I think he's scared."

She turned to me. "Come on. Class starts in a minute."

There it was, a picture of my life. I lose no matter what. If I hit him, I get locked up, maybe in my house, maybe in jail. If I walk away, Jake's friends win and I look like a fool.

I glared at Wesley. I stared at the crowd. Some of them backed away, nervous. I wanted to hurt them all. I wanted to make them bleed.

Libby grabbed my arm and pulled me to my feet.

"Let's walk," she said. So we did.

Chapter 8
Focus!

P.E.

They say it stands for physical education, but as far as I'm concerned it could mean "puny effort" or "puke easily." I ask you: Why should a person run in circles around a field? What's the point of climbing a rope or pulling yourself up on a metal bar?

I was pondering those questions later that day as I lay on the floor of the school gym, trying to do sit-ups while our P.E. teacher, Mr. Dudley, barked out a count from one to twenty.

That was about the extent of his ability with numbers, which was pretty funny considering the fact that he was also my math teacher.

He looked down at me. "Focus, Cray. Focus!"

I'd heard that Mr. Dudley had eight children of his own. I imagined him in the delivery room at the hospital, a kid under each arm, yelling to his wife, "Focus, Dudley. Focus!"

From the first day of class, Mr. Dudley had been convinced I was a slacker, and nothing I did could change his mind—until he found out I'd beaten up Jake Bragg. Then suddenly I was okay. He still yelled at me, but he didn't threaten to tear me limb from limb.

We finished our sit-ups, and Mr. Dudley gave us a quick lecture about the benefits of fresh air, multivitamins, and clean underwear. Then he told us to run three laps around the field and head for the showers.

Ah, the showers—my favorite part of P.E. It was a time when I could wash off the sweat, close my eyes, and stand under the hot water until any thoughts of Mr. Dudley dissolved, at least until math class.

Suddenly, running laps didn't sound so great. Hanging back, I waited for the others to head out, then took a shortcut to the locker room. The room was ancient, like the rest of the school, with lockers that were scratched and dented, wooden benches between them, and, high above, an old-fashioned metal ceiling fan that could never quite blow out the smell of dirty socks and B.O.

I ducked through the doorway, imagining hot water on my neck and shoulders. As I peeled off my T-shirt, I noticed a dark shape overhead. I thought of the shadows I had seen on my walk to school. Were they real?

This one was.

Dangling in the air was a mummy. Like every mummy in every bad movie, it was a human body wrapped from head to toe with white strips. In this case, though, the eyes had been left uncovered. Terrified, they blinked and begged.

The mummy writhed. There were muffled squeals and moans. Looking above it, I could see why. The mummy, like some hideous cocoon, had been attached to the ceiling by several of the white strips and was suspended high above the linoleum floor. One of the strips had been threaded between the metal blades of the ceiling fan, and with each turn of the fan, the mummy was hoisted higher and higher toward the ceiling. The fan's blades were rusted but looked as if they might be sharp.

"Hey!" I called. "Mr. Dudley!"

The mummy rose toward the high ceiling, spinning slowly as it drew closer to the blades.

"Mr. Dudley!" I yelled again.

He stuck his head out of the office. "What are you doing, Cray? You're supposed to be running laps." Then he glanced upward. "Oh my God."

"Come on!" I yelled. "We've got to do

something."

He stood there, staring. The mummy rose higher.

Gathering my wits, I raced around the room, looking for a switch to turn off the fan. I found it on the wall by the door, but someone had broken it off and taped it over. It could be fixed, but not in time.

"The fuse box!" I said. "Where is it?"

He shook his head. "I-I'm not sure."

The mummy was nearing the fan. Desperate, I turned to Mr. Dudley. "Give me a boost. Hurry!"

Finally snapping out of his trance, he ran over, clasped his hands together, and offered me a foothold. Taking it, I vaulted upward, braced my elbows on top of a row of lockers, and pulled myself to a standing position. The ceiling was a short distance over my head. Perhaps six feet away, the fan blades turned slowly, steadily.

"Be careful!" said Mr. Dudley.

Tell that to the mummy, I thought. It drew

closer to the blades, squirming desperately. Its blinking eyes were as big as basketballs. There were muffled shrieks.

Seeing the mummy up close, I realized its white strips were adhesive tape, the kind you use with bandages.

Mr. Dudley looked up at me. "Should I get scissors?"

It wasn't a bad idea, but the fan was too far away. Taking a quick inventory of the room, my gaze came to rest on a wooden push broom propped up in the corner.

"The broom!" I said.

Spotting it, Mr. Dudley raced over and brought it back. He held it toward me, and I grabbed it.

The mummy rose higher. It was just inches from the blades. I moved to the edge of the lockers and leaned out, holding the broom end and extending the handle toward the fan.

"Get under the fan!" I yelled to Mr. Dudley, and he did.

The handle didn't quite reach, but I had to do something. There wasn't time to think or plan or weigh consequences. There was only time to act—barely.

I lunged from the lockers toward the fan, jamming the handle between the blades and the ceiling. The fan shuddered, made a noise like a garbage disposal, and stopped. Unfortunately I didn't. I hit the mummy, hung on for dear life, and the two of us went plunging downward, landing on top of Mr. Dudley.

Stunned, we lay in a pile. Nobody said anything. Then Mr. Dudley smiled at me.

"Cray, you did it," he breathed.

I managed a shaky grin. "You told me to focus."

Chapter 9
Equal Rights for Thugs

It was Wesley Gault.

Funny how life works—the person I had most wanted to hurt just that morning had almost died. Someone had wrapped him in tape and strung him up. If I hadn't come in for an early shower, there was no telling what we might have found in the locker room.

After we had crashed to the floor, Mr. Dudley had hurried to the phone and called Ms. Fein, the principal. Meanwhile I had begun to peel away the tape, starting with the strips over the mummy's mouth. When they had come off, Wesley had let out a screech and whined, "I want to go home."

The rest of the class wandered in a moment later after running their laps. As they crowded inside the door, gawking, Ms. Fein pushed her way through. She was short and trim, a sharp dresser, with a voice like a bullhorn. It was strange seeing her in the boys' locker room. I had talked to her before, after the fight, when she had given me her thoughts about what I had done—basically, shape up or ship out. Oh, and if you need me, I'm here for you.

By the time Ms. Fein arrived, Mr. Dudley and I had peeled the tape from Wesley's face, neck, and arms. With each strip, Wesley had yelped with pain. When his hands were free, he had pushed us away so he could finish the job himself.

"What's going on here?" demanded Ms. Fein.

As she spoke, I noticed a familiar figure behind

her. He wore a police uniform and a skeptical expression. It was Sergeant Clark.

"Hello, David," he said. "You're one busy kid."

"I didn't do this," I said.

Mr. Dudley agreed. "He may have saved Wesley's life. Of course, the only reason he was here to do it was that he had ditched class."

"I hate laps," I said.

"You hate lots of things," said Clark.

Wesley looked up from the tape. "He beat up my friend."

Clark furrowed his brow. "Jake Bragg is your friend?"

"Yes, sir."

I had never heard Wesley Gault call anybody "sir," but I decided this wasn't the time to point it out.

Clark studied me then squatted down beside Wesley. "Okay, son, you want to tell us what happened? Start at the beginning."

According to Wesley, he had been late for class

that morning, and as he was hurrying down an empty hallway, someone had grabbed him from behind and pulled him into a supply closet. The person had wrapped him with tape, tied a handkerchief over his eyes, and left him there for what seemed like a long time. When the person had come back, he had carried Wesley to the locker room and lifted him up high. At first, all Wesley knew was that he was spinning.

Then the person had removed the handkerchief, and Wesley had realized he was dangling from the fan, moving higher and higher toward the blades.

"Did you see who did it?" asked Clark.

Wesley shook his head. "I never heard him either. He didn't talk."

Ms. Fein snorted. "How do we know it was a him? Women do bad things too."

What a concept. Equal rights for thugs.

I looked around for clues—anything that might help us figure out who had done it. Lying on a bench nearby was a sheet of paper. I picked up the paper. On it, words were printed in blocky, handwritten letters.

> Over the land, under the sea,
> Look all around but you won't find me.
> Crouching in corners, hiding in one.
> Plenty of pain. Plenty of fun.
> —The Raven

The money burned like an ember in my pocket. Desperate to keep it from Reynolds, I fled.

But where could I go? There was just one answer.

When Ginny and I had lived in Baltimore, a man named Kennedy had befriended me. No, not a man—a saint! He had set up a room for me in his house, where I wrote some of my finest stories.

Now I went to him again. Seeing my woeful condition, Kennedy begged me to come inside, but I declined. I gave him my money for safekeeping and staggered off to the opium dens.

Two days later, I awoke to find myself in a hospital, dying.

Believe me when I tell you this: it wasn't death I feared. I welcomed it. I would be joining my sweet Ginny. What terrified me was burial.

Can you imagine it? Trapped beneath tons of dirt. The air seeping out. The worms creeping in. The demons eyeing me, cracking their knuckles. I could not bear the thought.

So I devised a plan.

Chapter 10
A Weird Coincidence

"Who's the Raven?" asked Libby.

By the time school was out, she and every other student at Marshall knew what had happened. The rest of my P.E. class had seen the whole thing, and I noticed that a couple of periods later, in band rehearsal, wild versions of the story had begun to circulate.

Thankfully, none of the stories involved me. They focused on the mysterious Raven and overlooked the fact that I'd been there at all.

Finally, to control the rumors, Ms. Fein had made an announcement and given the basic facts. She had even posted a copy of the poem on the bulletin board outside her office, in case anyone recognized the writing.

Libby had crowded around it along with everyone else. I didn't need to. I could see it every time I closed my eyes.

On the way home, she had asked about the Raven.

I shrugged. "How should I know?"

"Oh, come on, David. Surely you've thought about it. There's a raven at your house."

I remembered the dream and the way the raven's eyes had glowed, washing the room in blood. For a moment, I wondered if the blood was spreading. I shook my head, and the dream dissolved.

"That's totally different," I said. "It's a carving."

"You've got to admit, it's a weird coincidence.

"My whole life is weird," I said. "Why should

this be any different?"

She said, "It's just so strange. A mummy? A note?"

"I'll tell you what's really strange—poetry in the boys' locker room."

"I'm serious," she said. "Don't you wonder who the Raven might be?"

Truthfully, it was all I'd thought about since P.E. class. I decided to share a few of my ideas. Maybe Libby would have some of her own.

"I think it's a guy," I said. "He was strong enough to grab Wesley, wrap him up, and somehow hang him from the ceiling. That would have been tough. Plus, he had to know about the fan. He must have been in the boys' locker room scouting it out. I don't think a girl would have done that."

"Makes sense," said Libby. "What about this? The note was written by someone who likes puzzles. He wants us to figure it out. It's like...he's taunting us."

"And threatening us," I said. "'Plenty of pain.

Plenty of fun.'"

Libby nodded. "He's creepy, but he likes to write. He's good at it."

"I agree. He's smart and dangerous."

"Did the police say what they'll do?" asked Libby.

"Sergeant Clark told me they don't have much to go on. There were no fingerprints on the locker or in the room."

She shivered. "I'm worried."

I put my arm around her shoulders. It felt good.

"You think more will happen?" she asked.

I had to be honest. I was getting a bad feeling about this.

"Yeah," I said. "Don't you?"

* * *

The Raven didn't know it, but in a way he had helped me. At school I'd been the bad guy, the kid who had sent Jake Bragg to the hospital. Now there was a new bad guy. Suddenly everyone was talking about the Raven.

He had helped me at home too. Ms. Fein no-
tified our parents and told them everything was
fine, but my mom had her doubts.

"This person, the Raven," she said after school
that day. "They're still trying to catch him?"

"That's what Sergeant Clark told us," I said.
"They're working on it."

My mom had started biting her nails again,
a sure sign she was worried. "With him running
around loose, I don't like the idea of you spending
your afternoons alone at home."

Neither did I. When I'd first discovered the
room, stories had poured out of me, and I couldn't
wait to go back. Ever since my dream when the
clock struck twelve, the torrent had stopped, and
the room no longer pulled me in. I was wary of it,
almost scared.

She said, "If you don't go home after school,
why don't you come to the library?"

It was my mom's office, but as far as I was
concerned, it belonged to me too. Before I'd

started beating up bullies, reading had been my favorite hobby.

"Can I bring a friend?" I asked.

She glanced up at me, surprised. Ever since we had moved, she'd been encouraging me to meet people.

"Sure," she said. "That would be fine."

Chapter 11
A New Body with an Old Heart

The Enoch Pratt Free Library was a big gray building on Cathedral Street, just a few blocks from our house. It had that name because over a hundred years ago, some rich guy named Enoch Pratt gave the city enough money to start the downtown library and a few branches. At least, that's what my mom told me.

The lobby was huge, with pillars, mosaics, a

marble floor, and a skylight that made the place glow. In the center was the reference desk, where after school the next day Libby and I found my mom, helping a man look up some information. His clothes were tattered and he smelled bad, but she treated him the same as everyone else—with respect and a smile. I felt a surge of affection for her, and just as quickly a burst of anger at my dad. How could he leave her? How could he hurt her like that?

When she finished, she looked up at me. "Hi, sweetie."

"Uh, Mom—"

That's when she noticed Libby. "Oh, hello."

"This is Libby Morales," I told her. She started to giggle.

Over many years of practice, my mom has perfected a series of techniques for embarrassing me in any situation. Calling me sweetie had been a good start. Giggling at my friend was even better. What was next—baby pictures of me naked in the bathtub?

"I'm sorry," she told Libby. "It's just that when David asked to bring someone with him, I assumed it would be a boy."

Libby looked over at me. "You turn bright red when you blush."

"He's always been that way," said my mom.

Great. They were comparing notes, like lab partners in a science experiment. Trying to change the subject, I told my mom about Libby and the shop her father had.

"I've seen that place," said my mom. "It's cute."

Libby said, "My dad can fix anything."

"I'll come by tomorrow," said my mom. "I've got two chipped nails and a broken heart."

My mother, the comedian. I felt my face grow redder.

"So," said my mom, looking back and forth between Libby and me, "are you two doing homework?"

"We finished that already," said Libby, "but you could help us with something else."

She could?

Libby said, "I was wondering about your house. It's such an interesting old place. You think the library might have information about it?"

"Upstairs on the second floor," said my mom. "It's the Maryland Room, the local history collection. If we have information, that's where you'll find it."

She turned to help someone else, and Libby headed for the stairs. I followed.

"What was that all about?" I asked her.

"The Raven is out there, and we need to find him," said Libby. "Your house may be part of it."

"Oh, come on. Because of the carving?"

"It's the only lead we have. Besides, it's such a strange old place. Aren't you curious?"

I had to admit, I was.

In the Maryland Room, we found some old maps of the downtown area and learned that our neighborhood had been there for over two hundred years. The photo file even had some pictures.

One of them, taken in the 1860s, showed what was supposed to be my block.

The funny thing was, my house wasn't there. I found where it should have been, and there was a different house, a big dark place made of bricks.

We asked the librarian about it. He was Mr. Knox, a friend of my mom's who was old enough to have taken the picture. I remembered him from a staff Christmas party we'd gone to when I was little. You may not believe it, but librarians throw great parties. This one was based on *A Christmas Carol* by Charles Dickens. Mr. Knox came dressed as Scrooge. And who played the part of Tiny Tim, with smudged cheeks and a little crutch? That's right. Even back then, my mom loved to embarrass me.

Mr. Knox, as much a historian as a librarian, studied the picture. "Sure, I know that neighborhood. So you live there, huh? They replaced those buildings in the 1870s. Built new homes and stores."

It sounded funny to hear my house referred to as new. I pointed to the old house in the picture. "When do you think this place was built?"

Mr. Knox scratched his chin. "If I had to guess, I'd say the early 1800s. The architecture is federal style."

Something caught my eye. Remember the mystery chimney on my house, the one that didn't seem to have a fireplace? It had unusual brickwork with a diamond pattern. That same chimney was on the house in the picture, I was sure of it.

I showed Libby, and she turned to Mr. Knox. "When they tear down an old house and build a new one, do they ever keep the chimney?"

"Sometimes."

I could see where she was headed. "If they used the chimney," she went on, "they'd probably keep the fireplace too, right?"

"I suppose," he said.

"So," said Libby, "you could have a new house built around part of an old one."

"A new body with an old heart," I murmured.

Libby shot me a look. I didn't say anymore. I didn't have to. We were thinking the same thing. If my house was built around the old chimney and fireplace, maybe it was also built around an old room. It would have been difficult to do, especially with a second-floor room, but it might be possible.

She said, "Could we find out who lived in that house?"

"Sure, if we have the address," said Mr. Knox.

I gave it to him, and he shuffled over to a shelf of fat books. They were city directories, listing names and addresses in a time before telephones. He looked up the address, starting in the late 1800s and going back as far as 1825.

"Well, I'll be," he said.

"What?" said Libby.

"It appears that your house was built by John Pendleton Kennedy. He also owned the house before it—the one in the picture."

"You know who he was?" I asked.

"Of course. So does any Baltimore historian worth his salt. He was Secretary of the Navy and a member of Congress. But around here, the thing he's most famous for is writing—not his own, but someone else's."

"I don't understand," said Libby.

"In the 1830s, Kennedy was one of three judges in a writing contest held by the *Baltimore Saturday Visiter*, a local magazine. The winner was a strange, penniless young man none of them had ever heard of. His story was called 'MS. Found in a Bottle.' Like most of the young man's stories, it showed a fascination with death and horror. Kennedy not only helped to launch the young man's career; he became a friend and mentor."

I thought of my house, built around a room from the old house. Someone had worked in that room, in a time before electricity and ballpoint pens. Maybe Kennedy, as a friend and mentor, had let the young man use the room for writing. It would explain a lot—the desk, the quill pen, the lantern. It might even explain why, when I sat in the chair, thoughts bombarded me and words poured out.

"This writer," I said. "What was his name?"

Mr. Knox raised his eyebrows and said, "Edgar Allan Poe."

Chapter 12
More Like a Coffin

The room started to spin. Mr. Knox flashed by, like a painted face on a merry-go-round.

"I need to be going," I mumbled.

"Me too," said Libby.

Mr. Knox watched as we left the room. Ducking into the hallway, Libby looked over at me. Her face was pale. "Do you realize what this means?"

"Yes," I said. "I'm going insane."

She said, "The room, the desk, the lantern, the

pen—those are hard enough to believe. But the carving!"

I nodded dully. "A raven. Like the famous poem."

"With the author's initials in the base," said Libby. "E. P.—Edgar Poe."

"It must be true," I said. "Edgar Allan Poe worked in that room."

We stared at each other. Suddenly I needed to know more.

"Come on," I said.

I didn't own a computer, but the library had a room full of them. We sat down at one, opened a browser, and typed Poe's name. A long list of references popped up, pages of them. We picked a few and started reading.

An hour later, we knew a lot more. You've heard the term misunderstood genius? That was Poe. People thought he was crazy. Maybe he was, but he had reason to be. His life was one disaster after another. His parents died when he was little, and he was raised by a man who grew to hate him. Later, when he started writing, his work was so strange and different that he had trouble getting it published, so he worked as a bricklayer and took on other odd jobs. Through it all he kept writing, virtually inventing three kinds of stories that are popular today: science fiction, mystery, and horror. His one big success was "The Raven," a poem with the famous line "Nevermore!" But he wasn't able to enjoy the success. His wife, Ginny, was dying of tuberculosis. Not long after she passed away, Poe was discovered, sick and delirious, on the streets of Baltimore.

No one knew what had happened or how he got there. It's still a mystery. The only clue was a name he kept repeating when they took him to the hospital: Reynolds. Four days later he was dead.

"What a sad life," said Libby. "Kennedy must have been one of his only friends."

"Poe was always broke," I said. "I'm sure he appreciated having a place to write."

Libby scanned the computer screen. "According to this, the writing contest was in 1833. That's when they met. Poe moved to Richmond a couple of years later, which means he only would have used the room for a little while."

"Kennedy must have kept it ready for him," I added, "with a pen and paper and lantern. Maybe he thought of it as Poe's room—you know, the way parents keep a kid's room when he goes off to college."

Libby said, "Then Poe died just a few blocks from there. Kennedy must have been devastated."

"If we're right, maybe it explains the room in my house," I said. "When Kennedy tore down the old house, he couldn't bring himself to destroy the place where Poe had worked. So he sealed it off and kept it as a kind of monument."

Libby shivered. "More like a coffin."

I looked at the computer again. "Wait a minute. It says here that Poe didn't write 'The Raven' until years later, in 1845, when he was living in New York. So where did the carving come from?"

We considered that one for a while. Finally Libby said, "Maybe the idea was there from the beginning, before Poe ever wrote about it. You know? Like, 'The Raven' wasn't just a poem. It was something inside Poe—horror, evil, death."

I glanced at the computer monitor, where there was information on Edgar Allan Poe along with a photo. The photo caught my eye. Leaning closer, I studied it for the first time. Poe was a haunted-looking man, with a scraggly mustache and eyes that smoldered like coals.

"Wait a minute," I breathed.

"Huh?" said Libby.

"That face—I've seen it before."

She snorted. "Well, sure. We've been reading about him for the last hour."

"It wasn't on the computer," I said.

"I'm sure there are lots of his photos floating around. Maybe it was in a book."

I shook my head. "It wasn't a photo. It was something else."

Suddenly I knew. My breath stopped, and my heart raced.

Libby watched me. "What is it?"

I mumbled, "Impossible. Crazy."

"Just tell me."

"Remember my dream about the room? There was a body in the chest. You know, the one that opened its eyes, sat up, and reached for me? It was Poe."

Summoning Reynolds, I described my plan.

At the moment of death he would put me into a trance as taught by Franz Mesmer, halting me at the edge of oblivion. I would appear dead, but my spirit would remain, suspended over the void. In the trance, I would be told to awaken at the sound of a bell.

They would bury me—but only for a short time! Reynolds would sneak into the cemetery, dig up the coffin, and take it to Kennedy's house. There, with Kennedy's help, the coffin would be placed in the writing room where I had spent so many happy hours.

Then, the crowning moment. Listen and marvel!

They would lift the lid. They would ring a bell. And I would rise—not quite alive, nearly dead. Racing against time and a decaying body, I would write the greatest story of my life—my masterpiece, describing a trip to death and back. Afterward, I would return to the coffin and expire, content that I wouldn't be buried but would rest forever in the room I loved.

Why should Reynolds cooperate? Because I promised him a fee of one hundred dollars, to be taken from my roll of bills. I gave him a letter to Kennedy with instructions for payment.

Oh, brilliant plan! Oh, dashed hopes!

Reynolds had something different in mind.

Chapter 13
L Is for Loser

In our research at the library, we had looked up the location of Poe's grave and found that it was just around the corner from my house, near the brickyard, at the Westminster Hall and Burial Grounds. We went there after school the next day and found a marble tombstone with Poe's name and an engraved picture on it.

Gazing at the tombstone, I ran my fingers over his name. "I read that originally he was buried at the back of the cemetery. Later they moved him to the front, so tourists could see the monument. I wonder what Poe would have thought."

"You don't want to talk about it, do you," said Libby.

"About what?"

"The dream."

"What am I supposed to say?" I snapped. "The house is haunted? Poe floats through the halls like Casper the ghost?"

"Something is going on," said Libby. "From the time you walked into that room, things have been happening—you write those stories, you dream about Poe. It's all about him, isn't it?"

"I guess," I said, nervously eyeing the tombstone. "I don't know."

"Then you find that mummy in the locker room. There's a note written in verse, signed by the Raven. Poe again. Poe, Poe, Poe."

"Shut up! I'm sick of that name."

I didn't want to be there. Things were closing

in on me. I felt trapped, like a man in a grave.

"You should go to the police," said Libby.

"Yeah, right. I've cracked your case. It involves a coffin and a quill pen."

Libby said, "We don't understand it, but Sergeant Clark might. He could help us."

"He could put me in juvenile detention," I said. "Anyway, I can't explain any of this without showing him the room."

"So?"

"I'm not ready to do that."

She stared at me. "Someone almost got hurt. He could have died."

I'm not sure why, but I didn't want anyone else to know about the room. It was too personal. It seemed risky, dangerous.

"I'm sorry," I said.

As it turned out, there were other things to worry about. For one, Jake Bragg was back at school. He didn't talk to me, but I'd see him lurking in the hallways, watching. He would huddle with Wesley. They would look at me and talk, then Wesley and his buddies would circle, watching me, looking for an opening, like wild dogs around their prey. The dogs weren't very smart, so I was able to slip away. But they knew the scent of blood, and I didn't doubt, given the chance, that they would pounce.

Then there was the band. Made up of middle school and high school students, it was a big deal at Marshall, partly because our football team was so bad. The team was known as the Fighting Irish, but everyone knew it was a joke. They hadn't won a game all season, and that wasn't likely to change.

I'd taken a few trumpet lessons when I was younger, so my mom had convinced me to join the band to make some new friends. Big mistake. The rest of the trumpet section, most of them high school students, had been together for years and had no interest in welcoming a new member. Sometimes it was hard even to understand what they were saying. They spoke in a kind of code, where one of them would say a word or phrase and the others would laugh, usually at me.

A few days after our discovery at the library, I took my trumpet and hurried to the football field, where we practiced during lunch hour. I'd been dodging Wesley and his friends, so I may have been a little late. When I got there, Mr. McGill, the band director, was talking with the mascot, a former trumpet player named Buzz Albright.

Buzz was an important guy, or at least that's what he thought. Since we were the Irish, our mascot was a leprechaun, so on Friday nights Buzz would dress up in a green coat and a vest covered with shamrocks. He would run around the band when they made their entrance at halftime, leading cheers, pretending to direct, and generally acting like a big shot, which is hard to do when you're a leprechaun.

"What's going on?" I asked Toby Kim, a kid who kept a stash of science fiction books in the bell of his tuba.

"Mr. McGill's all excited," said Toby. "His big purchase came in."

Spread out on the field near the goalposts were some green-and-white signs to carry at the front of the band. The signs, shaped like ovals, were about four feet high, and each had a letter on the front: M–A–R–S.

"Mars?" I said.

Toby grinned. "I like it. The band from Mars. We could wear bug eyes and antennas."

Of course, the signs were supposed to spell Marshall. Unfortunately, the Dream Team had only four members.

I should tell you about the Dream Team. It was a group of girls who didn't play instruments but still wanted to be part of the band. Their job was to prance around the mascot, jumping, cheering, and wearing glittery outfits.

As we spoke, Mr. McGill nodded, and Buzz Albright, self-appointed boss of the Dream Team, directed the girls to pick up the first four letters.

Buzz was holding a gray cat, a neighborhood stray he had adopted. Tying a green ribbon with shamrocks around the cat's neck, Buzz had named her Lucky. Get it?

Mr. McGill turned to the band. "Okay, listen up. We need four more people to join the Dream Team. Since you'll be carrying a sign, you'll have to set aside your instrument."

Toby leaned over and whispered, "Translation: bad players only."

A drummer raised her hand, followed by a couple of girls who played the flute.

"Okay, we've got *H – A – L*," said Mr. McGill. "Who's going to carry the last *L*?"

No one moved.

"Come on, people," he said. "You'll be helping your school."

I murmured to Toby, "Whoop-dee-doo."

Mr. McGill didn't hear me, but Buzz did. He swung around, holding Lucky, and glared at me. Then a smile played across his lips.

"Here's an idea," he said. "Since David's so excited, maybe he could do it."

There were a few giggles. I felt my face grow red.

"No thanks," I said.

Mr. McGill eyed me. "You were late today. It wasn't the first time."

Behind me, one of the trumpet players snorted. "*L* is for loser."

Someone started chanting, "David's on the Dream Team! David's on the Dream Team!"

The others took it up. Soon the whole band was chanting.

My face was beyond red. It was on fire. There was a furnace inside me, and Buzz had kicked open the door. Embers glowed. Flames leaped out. I wanted to shove him in, next to Jake Bragg and my dad, and watch him burn.

Buzz grinned. Maybe it was my imagination, but Lucky did too.

"I think it's unanimous," said Buzz.

I was just a few feet away from him. I could swing my trumpet like a hammer. I could make him hurt, the way that I hurt.

Maybe he saw it in my eyes. His grin faded, and he took a step back. I moved forward, gripping my trumpet with both hands. It felt good. It felt right. I took a practice swing. Then I remembered my mom. I smelled the police station.

I lowered the trumpet and walked past him to where the signs were stacked. Picking up the *L*, I heaved it as hard as I could—over the band, over Buzz Albright, over the goalposts.

Field goal. Three points. Whoop-dee-doo.

"I quit," I said.

Chapter 14
It Could Be Acid

I was still angry about having to quit the band. I had to admit, though, it wasn't all bad. Now I could go to the football games with Libby.

Of course, football games at Marshall weren't the same as in years gone by, when the team had taken state championships and the big stadium had been full every week. These days, the end zone seats were empty, and there were more people on the visitors' side than on ours. A lot of the

Marshall fans, like Libby and me, were middle school students who liked the idea of going to a high school game. That Friday night, we watched the massacre from the tenth row.

"The half's almost over," I told her. "Time for the biggest play of the night."

"What's that?" she asked.

"Go long. Get burgers. Eat burgers. I'm calling it now."

As I got to my feet, she pulled a five-dollar bill from her pocket. "Get me one, huh?"

When I got back, the band was on the field. The Dream Team led the way. Apparently they had found their loser, because the final *L* was in place. I sat down next to Libby, and we dug into the burgers.

"Buzz Albright is an idiot," she said.

"You're too kind."

"They said you were going to hit him."

"That's a lie," I said. "I was going to wrap my trumpet around his neck."

"He wanted you on the Dream Team?"

I primped my hair. "What do you think?"

She said, "That's not funny. He was mean."

I shrugged. "I don't need those people."

She studied me. "Why are you so mad?"

"Do I look mad?"

"You know what I mean. You're fine. You make jokes. There's no problem. Then something happens, and you change. It scares me."

"Sometimes I think I have an evil twin," I told her. "Unfortunately, it's me."

* * *

Glass shattered. There was a thump and a wild laugh.

It was Saturday night. My mom and I had driven home from a day at the library, and after checking the fridge, she had realized we didn't have anything for dinner. She went to the grocery store, and I headed for the den, where I turned on my favorite TV show. Five minutes later I heard the glass break.

Whirling around, I spotted a broken window directly behind me. There was a jagged hole in it. Beyond the window, a dark figure hurried away.

"Hey!" I exclaimed.

Leaping off the sofa, I scrambled down the hall to the front door, yanked it open, and raced out into the night. The figure dove into an abandoned building across the street, and I followed.

My mom had always complained about the building being a safety hazard, and she was right. The door was boarded over, but it had been pulled away so people could pass through.

Inside, the floor was covered with broken glass and twisted metal. I ducked to avoid an exposed pipe, from which water dripped into a big puddle. Small pink-eyed creatures scurried across my path.

I looked up just in time to see the dark figure disappear around a corner.

"Stop!" I yelled.

The figure kept going, and so did I. He found a stairwell at the end of the hall and ducked inside.

When I followed, I heard footsteps pounding on the stairs above me. Laughter echoed off the concrete walls.

Leaning out into the stairwell, I peered upward, hoping to see him, and something splashed my face. Surprised, I stopped and shook my head. My eyes stung, and a panicky thought rose up inside me. It could be acid. It might be destroying my eyesight, eating through my eyeballs and optic nerve. Then I smelled something. It was beer.

There was another laugh, and a door slammed. Wiping my eyes, I raced up the stairs to the second floor and threw open the door. There was no sign of him. I did the same thing at the third and fourth floors, but it was no use.

He was gone.

Chapter 15
Libby Snores

I walked down the stairs, stepping around the trash. On the third-floor landing, I spotted a beer bottle. I picked it up and shook it. There was still some beer left inside. Breakfast of champions, I thought. A college kid had told me that once. It had seemed funny at the time.

Returning to my house, I went into the den and inspected the area around the broken window. On the floor, surrounded by bits of glass, was a rock the size of a baseball.

"David?" called a voice from the kitchen. "Can you help with the groceries?"

I looked up, startled. My mom was home. For some reason, I wanted to hide what had happened. Maybe I was protecting her. Maybe I didn't want her to worry. Maybe I wanted to figure it out myself.

"Just a minute," I called back.

I stuffed the rock into my pocket. As I stood up, my mom walked into the room.

She noticed the broken glass and asked, "What's this?"

"Huh? Oh, I was watching TV, and something hit the window."

Coming closer, she studied the pane and the bits of glass on the floor. "You don't think it was a prowler, do you?"

"Maybe it was a bird," I said. "Sometimes they fly toward the light."

"Really? A bird?"

I shrugged. "It could have been anything."

She went outside and checked the ground under the window. I went with her and pretended to help. As I did, I noticed a flash of white under a bush. I reached in and picked it up. It was a napkin from Faidley's, the kind they give you when you buy crab cakes.

"What's that?" she asked.

I showed her and said, "I must have dropped it the other night."

We kept looking but didn't find anything. Finally she turned and gazed out into the darkness.

I headed back inside. "Come on. Let's get the groceries," I said.

She followed, looking nervously over her shoulder.

As we unloaded the groceries, I noticed her sniffing. "What's that smell?" she asked.

"Oh, that," I said, trying to sound casual. "You know those beers you keep in the fridge? I accidentally spilled one."

She fixed me with a stare. "Have you been drinking?"

"No. Of course not."

"David—"

"I swear, Mom. Not a drop."

"Sounds like things got pretty exciting when I left."

"Not really," I said, looking away.

After dinner I went upstairs to my bedroom, called Libby, and told her what had happened. Of course, she thought I should contact the police.

I said, "I can't. My mom doesn't even know. She thought it might have been a prowler. Maybe it was."

"Oh, right," said Libby. "Just another coincidence."

"Well, it could be."

We said good-bye, and I went to bed. I had trouble sleeping that night. Finally I rolled over and looked at my clock. It was after midnight. Libby had told me I could call anytime, so I decided to take her up on it.

"Hey," I said when she answered.

I could hear her fumbling at the other end. "Huh?"

"Sorry to wake you up. I was just thinking about my evil twin. The one who gets mad."

"Hmm."

"You know, I don't like him any more than you do. I try to push him down. Most of the time it works. Sometimes it doesn't. I get this feeling, like a wave. I don't understand it. Nobody does. Except you. Libby? Libby, I really like you. I just want you to know—"

A low sound came from the phone. I guess you learn something every day.

Libby snores.

I died but didn't.

When I awoke, all was darkness. I was in the coffin! I couldn't see. I couldn't move. But I could hear. Reynolds was speaking. Oh, cursed voice!

He gave instructions. The coffin creaked like a gate, then was ripped from the earth and carried to Kennedy's house. I heard the front door open, and Reynolds spoke.

He read the letter and said he would take it to the police as proof of a grave-robbing scheme, causing a scandal and ruining Kennedy's reputation, unless—

Wicked, wicked word—unless! Like a fence. Like a cage. Like a coffin.

—unless Kennedy gave him not one hundred dollars, but the entire roll of bills. Hundreds!

Reynolds never described the trance. Never mentioned the bell.

Kennedy, desperate, demanded proof of Reynolds's story. Reynolds opened the coffin.

Light from a lantern streamed in. I could not move. I could not open my eyes. I could not cry out: for the love of God, wake me up!

The lid shut. The light went out. Darkness closed in.

Reynolds took the money and fled. Kennedy, horrified, put the coffin in the room and closed it off forever. It became my tomb.

I had tried to escape burial. Instead, I had suffered the most terrifying fate of all.

I was buried alive.

Chapter 16
I Nearly Threw Up

Libby was wide awake when I saw her Monday morning. I was getting some things out of my locker at school when I spotted her coming down the hallway. She was wearing the simplest possible outfit—jeans and a sweatshirt—but on her they looked great.

I wondered what she had thought about my midnight phone call. I'd been all set to pour out my guts when she had nodded off, a victim of my magnetic personality. Had she even noticed what I was saying?

As I moved toward her, someone screamed.

The weird thing was, it was a guy. You don't hear guys scream every day, especially not like this. It was as if something had been ripped from him— hair, lungs, heart.

Sprinting toward the sound, I spotted Buzz Albright standing in front of his locker. The door was open, and he was staring in horror, shrieking uncontrollably. My locker was close by, so I was the first to reach him. I looked over his shoulder to see what he was staring at.

I nearly threw up.

Inside the locker was his cat Lucky, or at least her body. Someone had grabbed her, pulled the green ribbon tight, and twisted.

A dozen other people crowded in behind me and looked.

"Oh my God," someone groaned. "Who would do that?"

Buzz hadn't noticed, but there was something else in the locker, a sheet of paper. On it was familiar, blocky writing. I reached inside and picked up the paper.

> The canvas is black. The brush is red.
> Painting in pain is my art.
> I'll sit and smile and wait a while,
> Then I'll cut out your heart.
> —The Raven

* * *

"The Raven strikes again," said Sergeant Clark. "What do you make of it, David?"

It was later that morning, after the pandemonium had died down. Word about the cat had spread like fire through the crowded hallway. Ms. Fein had arrived to find me holding the note, with Buzz still screaming in my ear. She had managed to calm down the students, then had called the police, asked the custodian to watch the locker, and escorted Buzz and me to her office. As we left, I had noticed Libby, a thoughtful expression on her face, watching me from across the hall.

Now, in Ms. Fein's office, I perched on the edge of a metal chair. Buzz Albright stood beside Sergeant Clark. Ms. Fein watched me from behind her desk, the way you might eye a spider in the bathroom sink.

"You were the first person on the scene," said Clark. "I just wondered if you noticed anything or saw anyone who looked suspicious."

I shrugged. "My locker was nearby, that's all. I didn't see anything."

"She was just a cat," said Buzz in a shaky voice. "Why would anyone do this?"

"Ask him," said Clark, nodding toward me.

I sat up straight. "What's that supposed to mean?"

"Whenever the Raven strikes, you're never far away," said Clark.

I stared at him. "You think I had something to do with this?"

"I don't know what to think. Both times, you were the first person on the scene. It's strange, that's all."

"We asked Buzz who might want to hurt him," said Ms. Fein. "He told us about your argument on the practice field. He said you were pretty mad."

I thought about Lucky, hanging there like a slab of meat. "Mad enough to kill?"

She studied me. I knew what she was thinking. I had tried it once with Jake Bragg. Next to Jake, what was a cat?

"Wesley Gault shoved you on the front steps of the school, and the Raven tied him up like a mummy," said Ms. Fein. "Buzz embarrassed you in front of the band, and the Raven killed his cat. Could there be a connection?"

As much as I hated to admit it, she had a point. I got mad, and the Raven got even. He had done what I wanted to do but was afraid to try.

The Raven was loose in the world, doing terrible things. Was he doing them for me?

Chapter 17
Thump

I hung around the house, drinking beer.

That's a joke. Actually, I couldn't have had any if I'd wanted to. After the window incident, I noticed that my mom had emptied all the beer out of the fridge. Thanks for the vote of confidence.

She had heard about the cat and the Raven, first through the neighborhood grapevine and then in a public announcement and a personal phone call from Ms. Fein. My mom doesn't scare easily, but I could tell this was getting to her. That night she pumped me for information, wondering why I'd been there, what I knew, and how dangerous it was. When she was finished, I trudged upstairs. I locked my bedroom door, went into the closet, and entered the room.

I switched on the lantern, and shadows jumped up all around me. They danced as I walked. I stood by the desk and remembered sitting there, writing as if my life depended on it.

Something had come to life and invaded my world. Whoever the Raven was, he seemed to know all about me. He was at my school and outside my window. He was just out of sight, laughing and thumbing his nose.

"What do you want from me?" I asked in a hoarse voice.

The wooden raven stared. The only sound was the floor creaking beneath my feet.

I left the room, closed the door, pulled the panel shut, and stepped out of the closet. I needed a friend, and it seemed that I had just one.

I tried Libby's phone, and she answered. Now the hard part: making sure she didn't fall asleep.

I said, "Crazy day, huh?"

"It was awful," she said.

"I wanted to see you afterward, but they took me to Ms. Fein's office. Sergeant Clark was there. He had gone over the locker. No fingerprints. Just that note."

"Who's doing it?" asked Libby.

I laughed nervously. "Sergeant Clark asked me the same thing."

"What did you say?"

"What do you think I said? I have no clue."

She didn't answer for a moment. Then she said, "Well, strictly speaking, that's not true, is it?"

"Huh?"

"The room—it's full of clues."

"That room is mine," I snapped. "Not yours or Sergeant Clark's or anybody else's."

Libby didn't say anything. Maybe she was

thinking about the broken window I didn't re-
port or the way I'd beaten up Jake Bragg or the
evil twin I'd told her about. I could feel him moving around inside me. He was angry, the way he
always was.

"I have to go," I said and hung up.

* * *

It was midnight on Friday. I hadn't slept well all
week. I had tossed and turned, angry at Jake Bragg,
Ms. Fein, Sergeant Clark, my dad—all of them.
When I woke up, it seemed that the clock always
showed twelve. Bells tolled in my head. The corpse
jerked to life and sat up straight. Sometimes it was
Edgar Allan Poe. Sometimes it was me.

The bedsheets were damp. I'd been sweating again. When did that start? When did all this
start? When would it end?

I had always liked the darkness. It covered
me like a blanket. I could pull it close and wrap
it around me. When I was younger I had used a
night-light, but no more. That night before bed,

like every night, I had closed the window and shut the curtains. My bedroom had been black as ink, like a substance, like a wall. No one could bother me. No one could make fun of me. I was alone.

Except I wasn't.

Someone was in the room. I'm not sure how I knew. I couldn't see him. I couldn't hear him.

"Hello," I said.

No one answered.

"I know you're there."

I lunged toward him. I got air. I thrashed around, trying to touch him, to grab him, but I couldn't.

He was laughing silently. I was sure of it.

"Shut up," I moaned. "Please."

Suddenly the room seemed cold. I shivered.

I could have turned on the light. I could have opened the door. I could have done lots of things, but I didn't. I sat there, staring into the perfect darkness.

It started as a feeling and became a sound, a

low thump repeated over and over again. It grew louder. The bed shook. The walls leaned in, though I couldn't see them. The sound crawled over me, wrapped around me, burrowed inside me.

It was my heart.

Thump thump. Thump thump.

When I woke up the next morning, the curtains were pulled back and the window was open.

Chapter 18
The Book Was Leaking

"How's Libby?" my mom asked at breakfast.

I looked up from my phone. "Huh? Oh, fine."

"She seems like a nice girl."

"She's okay," I said.

"Have you seen her since the football game?"

"Mom," I said, "it's not like she's my girlfriend."

"I was just wondering."

My mom was scheduled to work the weekend shift at the library. After the cat incident, she was more nervous than ever about leaving me home alone, so she asked me to come with her. I have to admit, I didn't complain. If I was going to spend another day staring at the walls, they might as well have books on them. Besides, I had a project in mind.

When we got there, I went to a computer terminal to check the library catalog. I looked up Edgar Allan Poe, then went to the shelves and found a collection of his stories. Settling into a big overstuffed chair, I began to read.

Two things immediately became clear. Poe was crazy, and he was a great writer. Reading his stories was like entering a dark cave, with water dripping and bats diving and small furry creatures brushing against your legs. Every step gave you a new view: a corpse, a candle, a bottomless vortex, a young woman whose face once was lovely but now was a skull. There were twists and turns, dead ends and drop-offs, deep pits and high ceilings. There was horror and beauty. There was everything you had ever dreamed of, if you drank too much and your father hated you and your mind was like a jewel but no one cared.

I read story after story: "The Murders in the Rue Morgue," "A Descent into the Maelström," "The Cask of Amontillado," "The Pit and the Pendulum." I started "The Fall of the House of Usher." As I read, flames leaped. Flesh burned. Screams overwhelmed me, and smoke filled my eyes.

Maybe the strangest story was "William Wilson." One of Poe's creepiest creations, William Wilson went to school with a boy who had the same name, the same appearance, even the same birthday—a virtual twin. The twin followed Wilson through school and into adulthood, tormenting him, haunting him, making his life miserable. Finally, unable to stand it anymore, Wilson turned on the twin and plunged a sword into his chest. The twin, covered with blood, looked up with Wilson's own eyes and face, telling Wilson he had murdered himself. I thought of my own evil twin. Did I have a William Wilson?

As I read, I started recognizing things. What I'd seen over the past few days began popping up in Poe's stories, reflecting my own life like one of those creepy fun-house mirrors.

First was the mummy. In Poe's story, it was jolted awake by an electrical shock, then blinked its eyes, shook its fist, and sneezed.

Then there was Lucky. Poe's cat was black, but its death was the same: hanging, strangled, one eye gouged out.

Finally came the nighttime visitor. In Poe, he sneaked into his victim's room and stood silently in the darkness. The sleeper awakened and moaned. The only sound was the beating of a heart.

They say the great thing about reading is that you can meet people and experience things you've never known. Whole worlds come to life on the page. They don't tell you the other part, though. After you've met the people and experienced the beauty and horror, you can close the book. You can go back to your life, sure that the monster with green eyes and fiery breath is shut inside the pages—flat, lifeless, harmless. Reading gives you danger without danger, pain without pain, death without death.

That's the way it's supposed to be. But in my world, the book was leaking. Terror seeped out. Blood ran down my arms and pooled on the floor. Misery filled the room like a fog. I wasn't just reading Poe. I was living him.

Suddenly panicked, I slammed the book shut. When I did, something moved. It was just a flash, a dark shadow at the corner of my eye. I turned, and it disappeared between the shelves.

After dropping the book, I jumped to my feet and hurried over to look. The aisle was empty. But through the shelves I saw movement in the next aisle. When I got there, it was empty once again. I kept looking, but he was gone.

I felt like a character in one of the stories,

doomed to chase a phantom for the rest of my days. The Raven, if that's who it had been, was still one step ahead of me.

One hundred sixty-five years.

Do you have any idea how long that is? Do you know how much longer it would be if you were trapped in the darkness, dangling between life and death?

Perhaps I went insane. Perhaps I was distilled, compressed, hardened like a diamond.

Mesmer, you see, had been right. Spirits have a life of their own. They churn. They quiver. They reach out, seeking the spirits of people and objects.

First was the carving.

In the days when I had hands, I had learned to whittle. To my amazement, a shape had emerged. It was a raven, big and ghastly grim. When I finished, I painted the feathers black and the eyes red. I kept it in the room, where it stared at me as I wrote. It was more than a raven. It was death itself, beckoning. It crept into my stories and later became a poem.

My spirit found the carving, black and terrible,

and lit it up from the inside. But it wasn't enough. I wanted more.

My spirit swirled. It reached out.

And found you.

Chapter 19
A Muffled Scream

It was called Four-Leaf Clover Day.

The idea came from Ms. Fein, who said she was sick of watching the Raven terrorize our school. To boost school spirit, she had announced Four-Leaf Clover Day, when students would be honored for special service to the school. The highlight would be an all-school assembly where awards would be presented.

I hadn't seen Libby for nearly a week, but when

I entered the auditorium on the afternoon of the assembly, I found myself looking for her. She was near the front, next to an empty seat. Gathering my courage, I slid in beside her.

"Hey," I said.

"Hey."

We stared at the front of the auditorium.

She said, "You know that night when you called me? You said you didn't have any clues."

"Yeah?" I said, bracing myself.

"I decided you were right. You really are clueless."

I glanced over at her. There was a hint of a smile on her face. Suddenly the day was a little brighter.

The mood was broken when an explosion rocked the auditorium. It turned out to be Ms. Fein tapping the microphone. "Is this thing on?"

After the traditional earsplitting feedback and a quick welcome, Mr. McGill pounded out the National Anthem on the piano, then Ms. Fein stepped back up to the microphone. It was on a podium at the front of the stage with closed curtains behind it. Ms. Fein was in rare form, like a drill sergeant with mascara.

Pounding the podium, she bellowed, "We are the Fighting Irish, and we will not be intimidated! Do you hear me?"

We heard her, but nobody said much of anything. It didn't seem to faze her. She explained how the idea of Four-Leaf Clover Day had come to her, then she began handing out little green trophies—lots of them. There were awards for leadership, school spirit, neatness, promptness, best smile, best braces, best shoes, best accessories. As she handed Arnie Goldman the award for left-handed penmanship, the curtains behind her started to open.

I leaned over to Libby. "The grand finale," I said. "This should be good."

The funny thing was, Ms. Fein kept right on talking, as if she didn't know about it. A moment later, I saw why.

The curtains drew back to reveal a large pendulum suspended by a cable from above, swinging from side to side across the stage, the way a pendulum swings in a grandfather clock. But instead of a simple weight at the end, there was a rounded blade, the kind you'd find on a scythe. The blade gleamed in the lights, and with each swing, it dipped a little lower. Beneath it, someone was bound and gagged, wearing a blindfold.

The crowd gasped. It was Jake Bragg.

As shocking as the sight was, it was familiar to me. A similar scene had been described in "The Pit and the Pendulum," one of the Poe stories I had just read.

Ms. Fein, finally turning around to notice, shrieked, "Everyone, stay calm!"

Without thinking, I leaped from my seat and raced to the front of the auditorium, with Libby right behind me. As we mounted the stage, I saw that Jake was tied to a bench with his arms at his sides, exposing his chest.

The blade swung again.

It hissed by, just an inch from Jake's shirt.

The place was in an uproar. I shouted to Libby, "Let's move the bench!"

We tried, but it wouldn't budge. I glanced down and saw that it had been bolted to the stage.

The blade swung again.

There was a muffled scream. The blade had sliced the shirt, and beneath it, a neat red stripe appeared on Jake's chest.

"What'll we do?" Libby yelled desperately.

We couldn't move the bench. There was no time to untie him. So I did the only thing I could think of.

The blade swung again.

I leaped, grabbing the cable above the blade and hanging on for dear life. The force of my jump pushed the blade sideways, so it whistled past Jake. As it swung away from him, I felt the cable give way, and suddenly I was falling. The blade hit the stage and stuck in the wooden floor, vibrating like a knife. I landed on top of the pendulum, where it was hard but not sharp. I ended up sprawled there, gazing dully at the audience, with the cable coiled in my lap.

Libby hurried over. "Are you all right?"

I grunted.

Mr. McGill was the first to reach Jake. Pulling out a pocket knife, he cut the ropes and pulled off the gag and blindfold.

Jake shook his head, struggled to sit up straight, and turned around to face me. Even though it was Jake, I have to admit I expected some kind of thank you.

Instead he screwed up his face, pointed an accusing finger at me, and yelled, "He did it!"

Chapter 20
Welcome to My Nightmare

"Are you nuts?" said Libby. "David just saved your life!"

Jake shook his head furiously. "Who else would do this?"

"Did you see him do it?" asked Mr. McGill.

"Well, no, I was blindfolded. But I know it was him."

For a second I thought Jake was trying to frame me, to get back at me for beating him up. Then I saw the look in his eyes. It was fear. What he was saying wasn't true, but he believed it.

Someone came hurrying over, and I saw that it was the school nurse, carrying a first aid kit. Leaning over Jake, she examined the cut on his chest.

"You're a lucky boy," she said. "This is just a scratch. Your shirt took the brunt of it."

She swabbed the cut with alcohol and applied a bandage. By that time, half the faculty had crowded onto the stage, led by Ms. Fein, who was trying unsuccessfully to restore order. As they milled around, Mr. McGill noticed a sheet of paper. "What's this?" he said.

He set it on the bench and smoothed it out with the side of his hand. Libby and I leaned over to read it, and Ms. Fein joined us.

Blood, blood everywhere—
This is what I love!
Dark pit down below,
Pendulum above.

Hands clench. Hearts pound.

Stomachs lurch and heave.

Welcome to my nightmare.

Now you'll never leave.

—The Raven

This wasn't an empty gesture. We were way past that. It was dark and twisted. It was evil.

Ms. Fein whipped out her phone and made a call, then threaded her way through the crowd and back to the podium, where she tapped the microphone.

"Is this still on?" she said. "Attention, please. Everything is fine. The assembly is over. Go back to class."

Turning off the microphone, she pointed at Jake, Libby, Mr. McGill, and me. "You, you, you, and you—stay here."

I glanced over at Libby. She moved closer, and her shoulder touched mine.

As the crowd broke up, I heard a siren in the

distance. It was a sound I was beginning to hate. A few minutes later, Sergeant Clark entered the auditorium. For some reason I thought of my dad. I wondered where he was and what he was doing, whose life he was making miserable.

Ms. Fein hurried up to Sergeant Clark and told him what had happened. He checked to make sure Jake was all right, then inspected the blade.

"It's as sharp as a butcher knife," he said. "Another swing…"

"David saved him," said Libby. "He jumped on the blade and knocked it sideways."

Jake said, "He hates me!"

"Then why did he save you?" asked Clark.

Jake looked from me to Sergeant Clark and back again. He didn't have an answer.

Mr. McGill handed the poem to Clark, who read it and shook his head. "The Raven," he said. "It figures."

"Who is he?" said Ms. Fein. "Are there clues?"

"I was just thinking about that," said Clark. He

turned to me. "David, help me with this. A student gets wrapped up like a mummy, and you find him. A cat is strangled, and you're there. A pendulum swings, and you're watching from the front row. If I had a brain in my head, which my wife claims I don't, I'd say it's obvious who the Raven is. Jake Bragg swears that he knows, and I'm starting to think he's right.

"There's no mystery here. The Raven is you."

Chapter 21
Oh, Shut Up

I gaped at him. "Me? You think I'm the Raven?"

"That doesn't make sense," said Libby. "Why would he do it?"

Sergeant Clark shrugged. "I'm a cop, not a psychiatrist. But I've seen it before. Some people attract trouble. They draw it to them, like a magnet. Some of them find out they like it. It's exciting. It makes them feel important. Maybe they start doing things—little stuff at first, then bigger. It's like an addiction. They have to feed it."

"That's crazy," I said.

Clark studied me. "The funny thing is, I like you. I always have. But I think you're one seriously mixed-up kid."

"So that's it?" said Libby. "That's your theory?"

"It makes sense, in a sick way," said Clark. "You wrap up the mummy, then save him. You hang the cat, then hurry over to help. Neat, huh? You cause the trouble, then get to be the hero. Like today. Hang the pendulum. Set up Jake Bragg, then rescue him."

I couldn't believe what I was hearing. "Ask Libby. I couldn't have done it. She was with me."

"When?" said Clark.

"This afternoon," I said.

He looked at Libby. "The whole time?"

"Well, most of it," she said.

"So, there might have been time for him to do this?" asked Clark. "Theoretically?"

"Sure, theoretically," said Libby. "But he didn't.

And he wouldn't. He's not that kind of person."

Clark said, "Okay, then, explain this. Of all the people on campus the Raven could have picked for this stunt, why did he choose Jake Bragg?"

I noticed Ms. Fein eyeing me. "Interesting," she said.

Jake pointed at me. "He did it!"

"Oh, shut up," said Libby.

I tried to appear confident, but inside I was shaking. Somewhere out there, the Raven was lurking. Wherever I went, he went. He thought my thoughts and dreamed my dreams. When I got angry, he struck back. Maybe, like William Wilson, I really did have an evil twin, and he wasn't inside me. He was outside, in the world, doing things I longed to do.

Sergeant Clark shook his head sadly. "Sorry, son, but I'm afraid I'll have to take you in."

"You're not serious. I'm under arrest?"

He said, "I just need to ask you a few questions, that's all."

My head was spinning. I didn't want to go to the police station. They would grill me, call my mom, maybe even put me in jail.

I looked at Libby. Seeing the panic on my face, she turned to Sergeant Clark. "We've got homework tonight. Can he at least get his books?"

I knew that we didn't have homework. When I started to say something, she poked me with her elbow.

Clark said, "I guess that would be okay." He nodded at Mr. McGill. "I have a couple of things to finish up here. Could you walk him over to get his books?"

"Sure," said Mr. McGill. "Let's go, David."

"I'll come with you," said Libby.

On the way, we passed the band room. Libby glanced inside as we walked by, then did a double take.

"Hey," she yelled through the doorway, "that's a clarinet, not a baseball bat!"

Mr. McGill skidded to a stop, pushed past

Libby, and lunged through the doorway. As he did, Libby grabbed my hand, pulling me around the corner and out the front doors.

I stopped on the steps. "What are you doing?" I squawked. "Sergeant Clark's taking me in."

"Are you the Raven?" asked Libby.

"Of course not."

"All right, then, having you in custody doesn't help anyone," she said. "In fact, people could be hurt."

"Really?"

"Think about it. You and I are the only ones who know you're innocent. If we don't do something, the Raven will strike again, and this time it could be worse."

She was right. Sergeant Clark wouldn't stop it. No one else would either. It was up to us.

I followed her down the steps and into the streets of Baltimore. Somewhere in the shadows, the Raven was waiting.

When you discovered the room, my spirit pounced. It inhabited you. It filled you with words. You didn't write those—I did! You were my hand, my pen, my bridge to the world. Oh, it felt good—years of stories, trapped inside, surging onto paper.

After a few days, though, I learned a surprising thing. The coffin had changed me.

Trapped inside, my spirit had brooded and festered. Inspired by the carving, I began to think of myself as the Raven—stronger, bolder, my strengths and flaws multiplied.

Writing, which had always defined me and satisfied my appetites, was no longer enough. The stories were pale and insubstantial. The characters, like me, were ghosts—wispy things, bloodless creatures you could see right through. I needed more. I wanted life itself.

I had to escape the coffin. All I needed was a bell.

Chapter 22
Something That You Fear

There was a laundromat across the street. We ducked inside and ran out the back, down a series of alleys until we were blocks from the school and Sergeant Clark.

"Okay, we got away from the police," I panted when we stopped to rest. "Now what?"

"Find the Raven," said Libby. "He's planning to do something bad—I can feel it. Where could he be hiding?"

"It's been over a week since this started," I said. "He has to be staying someplace."

"Could he be at your house?" asked Libby.

"In the room? I don't think so. I would have noticed something."

We were silent for a few minutes, thinking.

I remembered the napkin outside our window. It was from Faidley's. I remembered the beer bottle too. It seemed that the Raven needed food. Suddenly I thought of the abandoned building. It was so obvious, I wondered why it hadn't occurred to me before.

"I think I know where to find him," I said.

* * *

The abandoned building was dirty and broken. Across the street, perched on a hillside, the house leaned back and watched. Behind it, dark clouds rumbled by, threatening rain.

It was midafternoon when we got there. At school, classes would be winding down, though after the assembly I doubted many people were studying. As for the Raven, our homework was done. The pop quizzes were over. It was time for the final examination.

"He's got to be here," I told Libby, looking up at the building. "It's quiet. No one bothers him. And he has a perfect view of the house."

"I hope you're wrong," said Libby, shivering, "but I think you're right."

I pulled back the board that covered the front door, and we went inside. The last time I'd been there it had been nighttime, and I'd ended up splattered with beer. Now, in the daylight, I saw how truly filthy the place was. There was trash everywhere. Ants swarmed over it, and cockroaches skittered by. The windows were broken, and the walls were covered with graffiti.

"What a dump," said Libby in a low voice.

I put my finger over my lips. "He might hear us," I whispered.

Trying to move as quietly as possible, I led her up the same staircase I had climbed that night. On the third-floor landing, where I'd found the beer bottle, a note was taped to the door.

When you come in,
The fun will begin.

Libby and I exchanged glances. The color had drained from her face. We had thought we were smart to find him, but the Raven was smarter. He'd been watching us all along. He knew we were coming. More than that, it seemed, he knew what we were thinking.

For a moment I wanted to leave—just turn, run down the stairs, and never come back. If I did, though, people might get hurt. Besides, I knew he would follow me into my house and into my dreams. The only way to stop him was to face him.

Libby must have been thinking the same thing. She tilted her head toward the door and gave a quick nod. Whatever happened, we were in it together.

I opened the door. Inside, in an empty hallway, a dirty blanket was spread on the floor. Next to it was a flashlight, a box of matches, a half-eaten candy bar, and an empty beer bottle.

The Raven was nowhere to be seen. On the blanket was a note, written in the same blocky printing as before.

> Think of something that you fear.
> Think of someone you adore.
> Think of how you long to see her.
> Quoth the Raven, "Nevermore!"

"What does it mean?" asked Libby.

"That last line is from 'The Raven,' by Poe," I said. "He was referring to death."

"Is someone going to die?"

I picked up the poem and studied it. *Something that you fear. Someone you adore.*

"The house!" I said. Then I gulped. "My mom!"

Chapter 23
A Perfect Moment

Stuffing the poem into my shirt pocket, I turned and raced down the stairs, with Libby right behind me. We squeezed past the board covering the front door and sprinted across the street.

The old house loomed ahead like a giant tomb. We climbed the steps. I unlocked the front door.

"Mom?" I called. There was no answer.

We charged through the house, checking the rooms. When we finished the first floor, we searched the second, saving my bedroom for last. Peering inside, we found nothing.

I whispered to Libby, "Now, for the big one."

I grabbed a flashlight from my dresser and switched it on. We stepped into the closet.

I pushed aside the clothes and placed my fingers in the crack on the back wall. It swung away, revealing the door.

I imagined my mom on the other side, tied to a chair, with the Raven next to her. She was the picture of terror. As for the Raven, he started out looking like me, but his face slid away, leaving a space as blank as the paper I'd found in the desk. Who was he? Why had he invaded my life? What did he intend to do with it?

I turned the knob, and we entered the room.

No one was there.

Stepping inside, I set down the flashlight and turned on the electric lantern. Shadows jumped out at us. The quill pen was there, as usual. So was the carved raven. The floor was littered with ancient, yellowing paper. The clock stood silent against the wall.

I took the poem from my pocket and read it again. Libby peered over my shoulder.

"I don't understand," she said.

"Neither do I."

As I spoke, we heard a sound. It seemed to come from below us. Motioning for Libby to follow, I tiptoed through the closet and into my bedroom. There was another sound. Someone was downstairs. If it was the Raven, would he know we were here? I tried to remember if I had left the front door unlocked.

We heard footsteps, slow at first and then faster. He was coming for us. I scanned the bedroom, searching for a place to hide.

"Under the bed," I whispered.

We dove to the floor and slithered beneath the bed. The footsteps were outside the door. I was amazed at how quickly and lightly he moved. I was breathless with fright but couldn't help myself. I had to see what he looked like. Pulling back the edge of the bedspread, I peeked out. A shadow fell across the doorway.

My mom stepped inside.

She glanced around, taking in the bed, the dresser, and the rest of the room. If she noticed that the closet door was open, she showed no sign of it. Pulling out her phone, she punched a couple of buttons and brought it to her ear.

"Sergeant Clark?" she said. "I checked the house. He's not here. Yes, I'll stay put. If I see any sign of him, I'll call you."

She put away the phone, glanced around one last time, and left the room. We listened as she made her way down the stairs. Then it was quiet again.

We slid out from under the bed and stood up. Libby said in a low voice, "Your mom's talking to Sergeant Clark. He must have told her his theory."

"Great," I said. "Even my mom believes I'm the Raven."

"It's okay, David. We'll find him. We can do it."

"If he's not here, where is he?" I asked.

Libby thought for a moment, then said, "I think our best chance is that building. If we wait there, we can also keep our eye on the house."

I noticed that Libby seemed troubled. She tiptoed to the bedroom doorway, peered into the hall, and carefully closed the door. Then she turned to me.

"Look, David, I want to help, but I need to see my parents. The police probably called them too, since I was with you. I bet they're worried. I have to tell them I'm okay."

"Sure," I said. "Of course. You go on home."

She nodded, but I wasn't finished. "Libby, thanks for helping me. This is dangerous. You don't have to come back. I'll take care of it."

Her eyes flashed. "Don't talk like that."

I said, "It's my battle, not yours."

She reached up and gently touched my cheek. "That's where you're wrong," she said.

It was a perfect moment. In spite of the house and the Raven and all the bad things that had happened, Libby and I were together. For now, that was all that mattered.

She patted my cheek. "Let's get out of here."

I led her to the window and opened it. Just outside was the big oak tree. I shot Libby a shy grin.

"My private entrance," I said.

I stepped through the window onto a big branch, and Libby followed. We made our way toward the trunk, then scooted down and dropped to the ground. We crossed to the gate, pulled it open, and ducked behind a row of bushes outside.

"This is where we split up," said Libby.

I gazed up at the abandoned building across the street. "Come back when you can," I told her. "You'll know where to find me."

Nodding, she squeezed my hand. Then she was gone.

Chapter 24
Buried?

Suddenly I was starved.

It was as if, when I finally stopped moving, my stomach caught up with the rest of me. And I can tell you, it wasn't happy. Since lunch, I had saved Jake Bragg, escaped Sergeant Clark, run halfway across town, and searched two buildings. I figured the least I deserved was a sandwich.

The gas station up the street carried a few grocery items, and I bought a couple of flat gray things that could serve either as sandwiches or hockey pucks. I plopped down on the curb outside and wolfed them down.

It was the first chance I'd had all day to think. Maybe that was a good thing. Sitting there, I thought of all that had happened. It seemed that people were always leaving—first my dad, now Libby. I hoped she would turn out to be more loyal than he had been.

Shaking off the thought, I hurried back to the abandoned building. I pulled back the board over the door, stepped inside, and climbed the stairs.

It happened so fast that I didn't have time to react. One minute I was standing on the third-floor landing. The next, an arm gripped my neck and a knife gleamed at my throat.

"Hello, David."

It was more a growl than a voice. I strained to turn and see who was holding me, but he pressed the knife harder against my throat.

"Patience," he rasped.

"Who are you?" I asked.

"The Raven, of course."

His breath was hot against my neck. It smelled like garbage.

"Let's go inside, shall we?" he said.

He opened the door and dragged me into the hallway. The dirty blanket and empty beer bottle were still there. He gave me a rough shove. I stumbled, lost my balance, and fell onto the blanket.

I looked up, not knowing what to expect—my twin, a stranger, a monster? As it turned out, the Raven was none of those things. He had stringy hair and flashing eyes. A mustache crawled like a caterpillar across his lip. I recognized the face because I'd seen it in my dreams.

I gasped. "Edgar Allan Poe!"

"I hate that name," he growled. "Edgar is fine. Poe is good. But Allan—"

He spit on the floor, a yellow-black substance that bubbled and heaved. A bug skittered through it, slowed momentarily, and lurched on.

"Allan was the name of my foster father," said Poe, "a man who thwarted me at every turn. I visited him on his deathbed, hoping at last to win his blessing. He picked up his cane and beat me! The strokes were feeble, but by God they stung. I curse his name. I want no part of it. Edgar Poe—that is who I am."

I remembered the carved raven, with the initials E. P., not E. A. P. Now I knew why.

Staring at him, I blinked a few times, half-expecting the apparition to fade away. It didn't.

"This is impossible," I said. "You're dead. I saw your grave."

His lips curled into something like a smile. "Ah, yes, the grave. Impressive, isn't it? Beautiful cemetery, marble tombstone, thousands of visitors. At last my genius has been recognized. There's just one problem."

"What's that?" I asked.

"The grave is empty."

I shook my head. "There was a funeral. I read about it. They buried you."

He shuddered. "Buried? Don't utter that word."

"Well, didn't they?"

He lunged forward and grabbed my arm. His grip was strong and slimy.

"Yes," he hissed, "and burial was what I feared most. Shut inside a box, lying in the dark, trapped beneath tons of dirt for all eternity. I wrote about that fear—'The Premature Burial,' 'The Cask of Amontillado'—trying to kill it with my pen. It didn't work. The thought terrified me then and still does."

A drop of sweat trickled down his forehead. He swiped at it, his eyes wild.

"But," he went on, "I outsmarted them. I plotted it, oh so carefully. And it almost worked!"

"Almost worked?" I said. "What do you mean?"

He eyed me, then let go of my arm and stepped back, knife gleaming.

"Do you want to hear a story?" he asked.

You dreamed.

My spirit was there, managing, changing, channeling your thoughts. I pulled you out of bed and into the room that fateful night. I dragged you to the clock, and you started it ticking.

Midnight struck. The bells chimed—the bells, bells, bells!

Inside my head, something happened. The seed, planted in a trance by Reynolds that wretched day so long ago, sprouted and opened like a black flower.

I rose.

Oh, life! Oh, limbs! Oh, hands that could kill. Now I was the Raven.

I climbed from the coffin, into the world. And I discovered an amazing thing. My body—white, pale, withered—was suddenly strong. It had found a new source of power, a cauldron of heat and flame.

Your anger.

Chapter 25
Green Stuff Came Out

The Raven examined the knife blade, checking it with his thumb. Then he looked up, his eyes far away.

"The story began, as it ended, with death," he said.

His tale was as horrifying as it was irresistible. Starting with the death of his wife, he took me with him to Richmond and Baltimore, introduced the evil Reynolds, described the crippling pain, detailed his plan, and bellowed the betrayal that had buried him alive.

"And then," he said, "I discovered your anger."

I was back at Lexington Market, kicking Jake Bragg, watching him bleed. The thing I kept in the basement had burst free, and now it was loose in the world, staring at me through the Raven's eyes.

He said, "Your anger was beautiful—living, breathing, pulsing. Horrible."

The description brought an image to mind. "The dream!" I exclaimed.

He smiled.

"Terrible things were chasing me," I said. "There were worms and snakes."

"What else?"

"Skeletons. An army of them."

His eyes gleamed. "Right, right. Then what?"

I said, "Something inside me ripped. Green stuff came out."

"Yes!" said the Raven.

"The house sucked it up. There was an awful noise."

"That was me!" he shrieked. "I pulled you inside. I dragged you up the stairs and into the room."

I shivered. "I didn't like that dream."

"Oh," said the Raven, "that wasn't a dream. That part was real."

"Huh?"

He was gesturing wildly. His knife flashed in the dim light.

"Don't you remember?" he said. "Mesmer! He was right! Spirits hover. They reach out. Mine found you. It planted the dream, then hauled you out of bed and into the room."

"In real life?"

"Yes! I reached into your body and made you start the clock. It was all I needed. The bells chimed. And I awoke!"

He threw back his head and laughed. "Can you imagine? Alive again after a hundred and sixty-five years. After you were back in bed, I stopped the clock again, put things back the way they'd been, and escaped. For the next few days, I roamed the streets, shadowing you and observing your remarkable and appalling world."

As he spoke, I could see the excitement in his face. I imagined him following me through the streets, staring at cars, gaping at buildings. Then his voice dropped and his face fell.

"But there was a problem," he said. "I noticed that when I wandered too far away, my energy lagged. If I stayed very long, my skin wrinkled and my hair began to fall out. Then the awful truth occurred to me: Your beautiful anger, which had brought me back to life, was keeping me alive. It was the source of my power. I was its captive, tethered to it like a dog on a leash.

"It was a bitter pill to swallow. After all I had done to free myself—first from the grave and then from that grave with walls—I had come back to discover that I wasn't truly alive. I was still half-dead, a half-man doomed to a half-life.

"Filled with despair, I took up residence here, across the street from you. I considered ending it all. Then I thought of something I could do instead. I could create stories, but not the kind you scratch onto paper. These stories would be written in life. They would involve real people doing real things, and each would be signed with a poem."

"The mummy," I said. "The cat."

He grinned, revealing teeth that were brown and crooked. "Best of all, the pendulum. Do you see how brilliant it was?"

"You threw the rock through my window that night. You came into my room while I was sleeping."

"Thump. Thump. Thump." He threw back his head and laughed. "They were works of art—overtures, concertos, symphonies. Each one built on the last, going further, delving deeper. And now, for the grand finale, my greatest achievement…"

He wheeled and grabbed me. Holding the

knife to my throat, he wheezed, "We're not done yet. There's something else." He nodded toward one of the offices. "It's behind that door."

Holding the knife in place, he let go of my shoulders. With his free hand, he reached for my shirt pocket.

"What are you doing?" I asked.

He pressed the knife harder.

I said, "If you want money, you can have it."

I glanced down and saw a paper sticking out of my pocket. He pulled it out. It was the poem Libby and I had found in the building.

He grinned. "This will explain everything."

"No, it won't." I knew that in spite of what the poem said, my mom was safe. Of course, I didn't want to tell him that.

Smoothing out the paper, he read from the poem. "'Think of someone you adore.' Let's see, who could that be?"

My heart raced, though I tried not to show it.

He said, "You're a reader. You know words.

Think about that one: *adore*. It's a special word, don't you think? Not for fathers. Not even for mothers." He twisted his face into a sickly smile. "It's for that one special person, the one who brightens your day, who makes you sigh when she walks into the room…oh, God, it's enough to make you sick."

His face, suddenly dark, loomed over mine. I smelled his awful breath, and my mind was filled with pictures—not of the Raven, but of a person who had quietly slipped into my life alongside him, who had helped me stand up and fight him.

"Think of someone you adore," rasped the Raven.

I knew who it was. I dreaded the thought that he did too.

Pressing the knife against my back, he dragged me toward the office and kicked open the door. Inside, lying on the floor, was Libby.

* * *

The office hadn't been used in years. There was

191

an old metal desk and what was left of a chair. The window was broken and partially boarded up. A wastebasket had been turned over, and trash littered the floor.

Next to the trash, Libby lay on her back, bound and gagged. Seeing me, she pleaded with her eyes and struggled to get free.

"Let her go!" I said.

The Raven chuckled. "Oh, I could never release her. She'll be my greatest story, my grand finale, my *Mona Lisa*."

"What do you mean?"

"I'm going to kill her," he said. "And you're going to watch."

He hurled me to the floor. Before I could recover, he had slid in beside Libby and cradled her head in his lap. His knife was poised above her throat.

"Don't move," he purred. "Either of you."

Libby's eyes were open wide, staring at the blade. He lowered it to her neck and drew it gently across, never breaking the skin. At any moment, he could plunge it in. I struggled to my feet, wanting to help but not knowing how.

"There's a place on the side of the neck," said the Raven. "When you cut it, blood gushes out like water from a hose."

Libby closed her eyes. Her face was white and chalky.

The Raven coughed. As he did, his hand slipped, and the knife broke the skin on Libby's neck. He stared down at her, shocked.

"My darling, did I hurt you?"

I realized that for a moment he was speaking not to Libby but to another kind and lovely young woman, his wife, Ginny.

A drop of blood appeared on her neck, and he wiped it away tenderly. In that moment I saw a way out.

"Edgar," I said softly.

"I'm the Raven!" he said.

"Are you?"

"Shut up!" he said.

"The love of your life isn't horror or telling stories. It's Ginny."

"No!" he begged. "Don't utter her name!"

"Ginny—what a pretty word," I said. "It sounds like Libby, don't you think? Do you really want to hurt her?"

He gazed down at Libby, and in his face I glimpsed the fragile, troubled spirit of Poe, haunted by fear but believing, at last, in love.

I was surprised at how gently he laid her down. Then he lurched to his feet and pointed at me.

"I'll get you!" he said.

Moving to the door, he took one final look back. His eyes were sad. Then they narrowed, and his face contorted with rage.

"I'm coming back," he thundered. "You'll see!"

He staggered through the door and slammed it behind him.

Chapter 26
Hideous and Deformed

I hurried to Libby's side, cut the ropes, and removed the gag. When her arms were free, she threw them around me.

"I was so scared," she said, pressing her face against my chest.

I held her close. The Raven had been right about one thing. *Adore*. It was a special word.

We stayed that way for a while. But the Raven was still out there. We couldn't rest.

"Now what do we do?" said Libby.

It was a question we'd been asking a lot. Ever since the Raven had appeared, we'd been bouncing like pinballs from one decision to the next.

I said, "He's been one step ahead of us the whole time. All we've done is react. We have to change that."

"How?" she asked.

"Did you hear what he told me? He said, 'I'm coming back.' Remember?"

"So?"

I said, "Think about it. He needs power. And we know where he gets it."

She stared at me blankly.

"From me!" I said. "He has to come back. He has no choice."

"That makes sense," she said. "But then what?"

"We'll wait for him at my house. I have an idea."

"And your mom?" asked Libby.

"What about her?"

"She's at your house. She might be there when he comes."

I thought about it for a minute. Then, standing up, I reached into my pocket and pulled out my phone. I punched a key and waited.

"David!" said my mom. "Where are you? What have you done?"

The quiver in her voice told me everything I needed to know. She was scared—not just of what would happen to me, but of what I might do. Sergeant Clark had told her I was the Raven.

It was wrong, but it was something I could use.

"It's all Dad's fault," I blurted.

"What?"

"I didn't want to move. I hate that house. I hate the school. I hate him! I'm going to talk to him."

"Talk to him?"

"I'm on my way to New York."

"By yourself? David, no!"

"Sorry, Mom. I'm sorry about everything."

I hung up, then walked over to the window and

looked out.

"Now, we wait," I said.

Less than five minutes later, the front door of the house flew open, and my mom hurried out carrying a half-stuffed suitcase. She threw it into the back of the car, jumped in, and raced off down the street.

"That should buy us some time," I said.

"For what?" asked Libby.

"You'll see. Come on."

As we left the building, I noticed the sky had darkened. Clouds blew past the moon. The wind howled. Thunder cracked.

The house had changed. There was a fungus growing on the roof that had worked its way down to the windows. A yellow mist, hugging the walls, seemed to throb and glow. The house, like Poe, seemed to be changing into an evil version of itself.

We approached the front door, and I pushed it open. The hinges creaked. A hot breeze blew past us, smelling of mold and rot.

We stepped inside. Spiderwebs brushed my face, and I jumped back.

"Turn on the light," said Libby.

I flipped the switch. Nothing happened. I tried another one. The lights were out.

"When did that happen?" I asked.

"Maybe the lightning did it," said Libby.

I felt my way into the kitchen, found a pair of flashlights, and handed one to Libby. We turned them on and went upstairs. We checked the room. Everything was just as I'd left it.

Venturing forward, Libby moved the raven to the desk, then opened the chest. I joined her, and we looked inside. It was empty except for cobwebs.

"Think of all those years," she said. "How could he bear it?"

"He couldn't," I said.

I lowered the lid and moved around to the front of the desk, where I took the door key from the drawer and put it into my pocket. I told Libby my plan.

We went to the brickyard. It was down the street, just a block away. When we finished our work there, we went back to the house and made preparations. Then we waited.

"Where is he?" asked Libby.

"He'll be here," I said.

I stood at a window in the second-story hallway, too nervous to sit down. Libby settled onto the floor. She had spread a blanket in front of her and set out a few things from the fridge, trying to convince herself that what we were doing was almost normal, something you might take a break from to have a picnic.

"You want a Coke?" she asked, making herself a peanut butter sandwich.

I gazed out the window. "I'm not hungry."

It started to rain. The drops were huge. When they hit the window, they sounded like explosions.

In the downpour, something moved—like a shadow, but solid. Slinking along the street, it paused in the light of a streetlamp. It was the Raven. He was hideous and deformed, as if his body had been seized by giant hands and twisted. His back was bent. His head was turned at a strange angle and tucked down against his neck.

When he had left the building across the street, he had learned the awful truth: he needed me. Without my anger, his body would become twisted and then destroyed. My anger was what made him strong. We were chained together.

After finally escaping the chest, he was still trapped.

I nudged Libby. Switching off her flashlight, she scrambled to her feet and joined me at the window. We stood off to the side and peered around the edge so he wouldn't see us. He squinted up at the streetlamp, then turned away from it, limping toward the house.

A few moments later, we heard the front door open. The hinges moaned. The door slammed shut. There were footsteps—uneven, relentless.

Step, drag. Step, drag. Step, drag.

"David!" he roared. It was no longer a human

voice. It was the sound of fingernails the size of garbage can lids scraping against a fifty-foot blackboard. We covered our ears, but there was no escaping it. "David, I know you're here."

We gathered up our things, as we had planned, and ducked into a bathroom off the hall. We peeked through a crack in the doorway, watching and listening.

Step, drag. Step, drag.

His head appeared in the stairwell. Clumps of hair were plastered against his head. Rain dripped from his ears and nose. Shoulders emerged, then chest and arms. His hands were gray, and the skin was cracked. He grasped the railing and pulled himself up.

Step, drag. Step, drag.

He reached the second floor and looked around. His eyes fastened on the bathroom door, and for a moment, I was sure he had seen us. Then he turned and entered my bedroom.

We heard him inside. His steps never faltered.

He was headed for the closet and the secret room.

Step, drag. Step, drag. Step…step. Step, step.

The limp was gone. He was moving faster, already feeling the power. There was a click as he opened the closet.

I nodded to Libby, and we moved to the hall, where we peeked into the bedroom. The closet door was open. A light shone from inside.

We tiptoed across the bedroom and looked into the closet. The panel on the back wall had been moved aside, and light from the room came through the open door. Since the electricity was off, the Raven must have turned on the battery-operated lantern.

Libby touched my arm. I took a deep breath, stepped through the door, and closed it behind me.

Chapter 27
Grab Me and Gut Me

The Raven sat at the desk.

"Hello, David," he rasped.

I didn't say anything. He swung the chair around and glared at me. His face was dark, and his eyes burned like coals.

"You tricked me back there," he said. "You made me think of Ginny. That was a mistake."

"It seemed to work," I said.

His voice rumbled deep in his chest. "Maybe

for a few minutes. But not for long. Love doesn't last. Nothing does."

I said, "Whatever you're planning, you don't have to do it. You can turn yourself in."

He gaped at me, his mouth a bottomless pit. A sound worked its way out. It started as a low chuckle, then grew into a booming laugh. He slapped his leg. I noticed that the skin on his hand was smooth. The cracks were gone.

"Turn myself in?" he said.

"It's not too late. You haven't hurt anyone yet."

"So, that's your idea?" he asked. "They slap my wrist and set me free? Then what? I move in with you? We get bunk beds and eat popcorn on Friday nights?"

I shrugged. "I don't know. I hadn't gotten that far."

"So now we're here," he said. "What does your little friend think of it?"

I knew Libby had wanted to come into the room with me, but she seemed to realize that I needed to do this alone.

I said to the Raven, "Part of you is Poe. You can't be this bad."

He sat, watching me. He reached across the desk and stroked the carved raven.

"I used to get writer's block," he said. "Late at night, when I was working, darkness would descend. My hand and mind would freeze. So I took up carving. I found a block of wood and, sitting at this desk, whittled to pass the time. I didn't try to make anything. I simply wanted to stay busy."

He picked up the carving and set it in his lap. "It came out of my hands and into the world, like a story or a poem—already formed, poised in the ether, waiting to be discovered. It's death itself. It's in this room. It's watching and waiting."

He set the raven back on the desk. Picking up a letter opener, he cradled it delicately in his hands. Then, like a leopard, he sprang.

I had imagined that if he moved, it would be slowly, awkwardly. I hadn't counted on the energy he was getting from me. I thought I had learned, with Libby's help, to control my anger, but it was still there, trapped inside like the Raven in his coffin. The energy sizzled around him, making him quick and strong.

Realizing my mistake, I dove to the side, but it was too late. The letter opener slashed my arm. Pain shot through me.

I cried out. From the other side of the door, Libby called, "David?"

I scrambled on my hands and knees, trying to get away from him, but he was too quick. He took my leg and pulled, reeling me in like a fish. He was going to grab me and gut me.

I looked back at him. His stench was overpowering.

"David!" Libby yelled. "What's happening?"

"Don't come in!" I shouted.

He was pulling me closer. I could see his grin. I waited. I waited. Then I kicked the grin as hard as I could. Blood gushed from his mouth.

The Raven gurgled and snarled. He tried to hold on, but this time I was too quick. I jumped to my feet, grabbed the electric lantern from the desk, and raced for the door. As I dove through, I told Libby, "Shut it!"

She slammed the door behind me, just ahead of the Raven. I whipped the key from my pocket, jammed it into the lock, and turned it. The bolt clicked into place.

The Raven let out an unearthly scream. He was alone in the darkness.

Yes, I screamed. Wouldn't you?

Blackness. Nothingness. The void.

I thrashed around, desperate to leave, but the door was locked. The fireplace was sealed. The window was gone. After working so feverishly to get out—one hundred sixty-five years!—I was trapped once again.

I had escaped before. I could escape now.

I breathed. My breaths were ragged at first, then smooth and clear.

I made a fist. It grew stronger.

I had a thought. It became an idea.

All I had was my mind, my beautiful mind. And your anger.

Chapter 28
A Bloody Fist

Edgar Allan Poe had been a bricklayer. It was a job he could do in his spare time, between stories. Like everything else in his miserable life, he had used it in his work. So did we.

The bricks were stacked behind an old sofa in a corner of my room, covered by a blanket. Next to them was a bucket full of mortar and two trowels.

As we carried the mortar and trowels to the closet, Libby noticed my arm. "David, you're hurt!"

I looked down. My shirtsleeve was ripped where the Raven had stabbed me, and blood dripped out.

"I'm fine," I said but knew it wasn't true. The wound was painful, and I could feel it sapping my energy. I needed to see a doctor. Before that, though, there were important things to do.

I carried the bricks, and Libby laid them against the door, row by row, using a trowel to fill the mortar in between. We worked quickly, and soon the wall had reached our knees.

The Raven was busy too. We could hear him trying the lock, jiggling the knob, pounding on the door.

"David!" he shrieked.

Libby glanced at me. There was fear in her eyes.

"Keep working," I told her.

We heard a loud noise. The door jumped. I pictured the Raven on the other side, hurling himself against it. He tried again and again. The door was holding, at least for now. When we were finished, it would hold forever.

I wondered what it was like on the other side of the door. Once, when I first discovered the room, I had closed the door and turned off the lamp. My eyes were wide open, but the world had gone away. The only thing left was black, a black that was completely different from the color you see with your eyes closed. There wasn't a hint of light. There were no shadows or colors. A feeling of panic had risen in my chest. I wondered how long the air would last. I had trouble breathing. I imagined the walls closing in. Suddenly I hadn't been able to stand it any longer. I stumbled to the door and threw it open. Light poured in, and air.

Soon the Raven would have neither. He would never again see light. He would breathe for a while longer, then stop. He was trapped, about to be buried for the last time. I shook my head and tried not to think about it. The motion made me dizzy.

Bracing myself, I eyed the wall. Strong and

sturdy, it had reached the halfway point. Libby was working furiously. Mortar smudged her clothes and face.

I realized we hadn't heard the Raven for a while. What was he doing? Had he given up? I got my answer a moment later.

"David?" he said in a muffled voice. "David, listen to me."

I kept working.

"Think of all the people you hate," said the Raven. "Think of how they laughed at you, made fun of you, told you no. Wouldn't you like to wipe the smiles off their faces?"

"Ignore him," said Libby, stacking another row of bricks.

The Raven said, "You know what makes you weak? It's not what you would do—it's what you wouldn't do. You were weaker than Jake Bragg because you wouldn't hurt people and he would. Then something snapped, and you hurt him, badly. That's when he realized you were stronger."

I remembered the look on Jake's face. I knew the Raven was right.

"You and me, together," he said. "Imagine what we could do to the people you hate, just because we *would*. We would kick them. We would stomp them. We would watch them bleed. Think of it!"

For a moment, I did. Rows of my enemies lined up in front of me, and we cut them down like weeds. It felt good.

"David?" said Libby.

"Huh?"

I gazed into her eyes. They brought me back from a place far away, a place without light or air. I saw strength in Libby's eyes, but not the kind the Raven was talking about. Quiet and sure, it was a strength I could build on, the way we were stacking bricks, row by row.

The wall was higher now. It had reached my chest. As we worked, my arm throbbed. Outside, lightning ripped the sky. Thunder crashed. Behind the door, there was a different kind of crash.

"Hear that?" yelled the Raven. "It was the chest. I picked it up and threw it against the wall."

There was another crash. He let out a wild laugh. "That was the desk. I smashed it with my bare hands."

I remembered those hands. They had been gray and cracked when he arrived. After spending time close to me, they were smooth and healthy.

Libby whispered, "He's stronger. He's getting energy from you."

"Work faster," I said, handing her a brick.

We did, but it wasn't fast enough. As Libby laid in more bricks, the door above them exploded. Through it came a bloody fist.

Chapter 29
Talking to a Buzz Saw

The fist was huge, like an anvil.

As we gaped, another fist splintered the door. A jagged hole opened above our brick wall. Two hands seized the wood and broke it off, enlarging the hole. The Raven's arms, giant now, reached through the hole and writhed like snakes. Fumbling blindly, they latched onto my leg and seized it in a vicelike grip. Then they began to pull.

"David!" cried Libby. She grabbed me around

the waist and pulled back. It was like trying to stop the tide. I was going out to sea.

"Fight him!" said Libby. "Don't let him do it."

I pounded on his arms. I scratched them and made them bleed. I worked to pry his fingers loose. I braced my feet against the door frame, trying to get leverage. I grabbed at the brick wall, which was just beneath the jagged hole.

My feet went first. Then my legs, scraping against the rough edges of the hole, tearing my pants and cutting my knees.

Libby glanced around desperately. "What can we do?"

There was only one answer, but I knew she wouldn't like it. "Make sure the door stays locked, no matter what he tells you. And keep laying bricks to cover the rest of the door."

"But what about you?"

"Don't worry," I said. "I've got a plan."

"A plan? Are you sure?"

"Just finish the wall," I said. "You'll see."

The Raven gave a tremendous yank. My hips tore through the hole, then my chest, and finally my arms. Only my head was still outside, eyes blinking, looking around, trying to see into the future, if I had one.

Libby placed her hand on my cheek. "Don't go, David. Please."

Sometimes a lie is best. "I'll be fine," I said.

She leaned in and kissed me on the lips. I tasted peanut butter. Then she was gone.

Inside the room, I dropped to the floor with a thud. The Raven loomed over me, bigger than before. Somewhere in the darkness he had changed. My anger, nearby now, had turned him into something new and fearsome.

The room was still dark, but it wasn't black anymore. Light seeped through the hole in the door. Guided by it, the Raven fumbled around and found the kerosene lantern and a box of matches. He lit the lantern and held it over his head.

The place was a mess. The remains of the

chest were strewn by the door. The desk was a pile of rubble. Around it, sheets of ancient yellowed paper were scattered. Next to them, still in one piece, was the wooden carving, like a dark blotch on the floor.

The Raven set the lantern down next to it. His face was covered with blood. Behind him, a gigantic shadow danced on the wall.

"I'm glad you could join me," he said.

My arm throbbed. My legs and shoulders, cut on the door, had started to ache.

"Just tell me what you want," I said.

He grinned. Some teeth were missing where I had kicked him. "Oh, I have big plans. Let's see, there's Libby. Then your mother. Then that withered-up witch, Ms. Fein. Mr. McGill, of course. And Jake Bragg—I've got special plans for him."

"All those people?" I said. "Why do you want to hurt them?"

It was like talking to a buzz saw. The blade

whirred. It moved forward. Nothing you could say would change it.

My expression must have shown how I felt. The Raven saw me and snorted.

"Get used to it," he said. "I'll be doing a lot more. And here's the best part: you're going to help me."

For a moment I felt panic rising. Then I remembered.

"Oh, really?" I said. "How do you plan to get out of here?"

He smiled. "The way you came in. Through the hole in the door."

"What hole?" I asked.

He whirled around. Where the hole had been, there was now a wall. Libby had bricked us in.

The buzz saw shrieked. It echoed around the room. In two quick steps, the Raven was at the door. Reaching through the hole, he pummeled the wall. It held fast.

"Quick-dry mortar," I said. "It's amazing what

you can buy these days."

He turned back, a look of genuine puzzlement on his face. "Now you're trapped. We're both trapped."

I shrugged, trying to look better than I felt. My arm ached. So did everything else. "Okay, I admit it's not what I planned. I wanted to brick you in. You were going to die alone. Now I guess there'll be two of us."

"What about Libby?" he asked. For just a moment, there was a glimmer of something in his eyes.

"I think she'll understand," I said. "I hope she will."

The glimmer faded. Now there was only anger, red and ugly, evil, pulsing. Screaming with fury, he threw himself against the door. He pounded the bricks. He picked up a chair leg and paced the room, checking the wall for weak places. When he thought he had found one, he attacked it. He made a few dents but nothing more. The room held firm, as it had for almost two hundred years.

The Raven sat down heavily on the floor.

"It's just you and me," I said, talking as much to myself as to him. "But then, when you think about it, it's been that way from the beginning. We're trapped together. We're paying the price for what we've done. I beat up Jake Bragg. I can't change that. The things you did—the mummy, the cat, the pendulum—they're no different, really. They're more dramatic. They're based on your stories. But they came from my anger. They're still me."

The Raven lifted his head. "So, that's it," he rumbled. "It's over. Everything I've tried to do comes down to this. Pain. Death."

He stared off into space, then looked at me. "There's only one problem."

"What's that?" I asked.

"I'm still mad."

He got to his feet. Picking up the chair leg, he swung it into his palm, a little harder each time. Whack! Whack!

"When you're angry, you need a target," he

growled. "There's just one left."

He moved forward.

For some reason I thought of my mother. After I'd beaten up Jake Bragg, she had sat me down and told me that if I didn't change, my anger would kill me. Little did she know.

She had stood over me that day, her face red and her fists clenched. It seemed that I wasn't the only one with a temper. But she had used hers, not to hurt me but to help me. You could turn your anger on others, the way I'd done, the way the Raven had done, or you could grab it, pull it close, and make it a part of yourself.

The Raven was wrong. You didn't need a target. You didn't need someone to hate. You needed someone to love, someone you weren't afraid to yell at, the way my mother yelled at me, because you wanted to make them strong. With that thought, something in me settled into place.

Maybe I was about to die, but I felt calm for the first time in days.

As the Raven approached, he hesitated. He studied my face. Then he leaped. I dove to the side, accidentally bumping the lantern and tipping it over. Kerosene poured out, followed by flames. Fire raced along the floor.

I scrambled to a corner. The Raven, distracted for a moment, gaped at the flames.

The fire reached a pile of papers and exploded. It spread to the stack of kindling that was the desk. We were facing an inferno.

The Raven turned to me. He was black, silhouetted against the red flames.

"You did this!" he roared. "You ruined everything."

He came toward me. Trapped in the corner, I had nowhere to go. He grabbed my arm where it was bleeding. He squeezed. Pain shot through me, and I moaned.

"It started with Jake Bragg," he said. "It'll end with you. I'll beat you bloody. And this time, I'll finish the job."

I tried to back away, and he laughed. "You're going to die anyway. Let's go out in style."

He plowed his fist into my stomach. I doubled over. I couldn't breathe. He threw a vicious uppercut to my chin. There was a crack, and my jaw went numb.

As he drew back his fist again, the fire advanced, drawn to him like a heat-seeking missile, like hornets to a nest. It found the ragged cuffs of his pants, and his lower body burst into flame.

He stared down at himself. The flames spread to his shirt. Sparks shot to the sky.

"Help me!" he shrieked as his hair caught fire.

I reached out, but the flames were too hot. I stepped back. His face was gone, hidden behind a mask of fire. As I watched, he burned bright, a Roman candle with legs. He jumped and danced around the room. Then, with a loud *woosh*, he shriveled up and turned black. A moment later, all that was left were cinders.

Inside me, something stirred. It was anger. I

could use it. I didn't want to die.

I had read somewhere that in a fire, the best place to find oxygen is on the floor. I lay down, coughing, trying to breathe. The air was hot. It scorched my chest and lungs.

I closed my eyes and thought of Libby.

Chapter 30
Glue and Paint

She came to me in a dream.

I studied her face. It was kind. It was sweet and stubborn. It was honest, a face you could trust. I gazed at her for a long time. She gazed back. When I touched her, I noticed that her lips were moving.

There were sounds in the distance. One of them was her voice, far away. "David?"

Behind her, the house leaned toward me. The shutters were open. Flames licked out. The house was coming for me, I was sure. This time it would get me.

"David, are you all right?"

The sounds got louder. There were sirens, door slams, people shouting, dogs barking.

I remembered another sound. I had been lying on the floor, and the wall had exploded. Through the hole came firefighters, swinging axes and sledgehammers. One of them leaned down, picked me up, and threw me over his shoulder. As he dove back through the hole, the house lurched. It bounced as he took the stairs two at a time. A moment later I was outside, under a streetlamp on the sidewalk, and Libby was with me.

I looked up at her, blinking.

"What happened?" I asked. As I spoke, pain shot through my jaw.

"That was a great plan you had," she snapped. "Close off the room. Set a fire. Die."

I said, "That wasn't exactly it."

"Then tell me."

I shrugged. It hurt my arm. "Well, at least the fire wasn't planned."

"You are such an idiot," she said. "So am I."

Libby told me she had smelled smoke. She had called the fire department, which luckily was just around the corner.

We turned and gazed at the house. It was consumed by flames, lighting up the block as bright as day. The firefighters, wrestling hoses, shot water onto the house, but you could tell there was no hope of saving it. Fire engines surrounded the place, and beyond them milled a crowd of people.

As we watched, there was a crash and the roof caved in. One wall collapsed, then another. The flames leaped up. In them, it seemed to me that a face appeared. It had a broad forehead, cavernous eyes, and a stringy mustache. It gazed at us, smiled, and melted away.

"Did you see that?" asked Libby.

"I'm not sure," I said. "I'm not sure about any of it."

The house settled back and trembled. Then it came crashing in on itself in a great orange cloud.

* * *

They took me to the hospital, where they checked my jaw, stitched up my arm, and gave me oxygen. The oxygen felt good. In some ways it was the first fresh air I'd breathed for weeks.

Later that night, after Libby had gone, my mom came storming into the hospital room. She had been halfway to New York when they had called her. Her reaction was about what I would have expected. She yelled at me, then hugged me within an inch of my life.

I apologized for lying about going to see my dad. I told her I'd wanted some time at home to figure things out, and I'd known she would follow me to New York. As for the fire, I gave the story that Libby and I had agreed to—when the electricity went out, I had lit a kerosene lantern, and that's what had started the fire. We had escaped, but in the process my arm and jaw had been hurt.

It was true, as far as it went. She peppered me with questions, but in the end she was just happy I was all right.

Afterward, we talked about what to do now that the house was gone. Everything we owned had been destroyed—our clothes, furniture, family albums. I remembered a special photo of my dad and realized I would miss it.

Sergeant Clark came by the next morning. He had some questions about the fire, and I gave him the same story I'd told my mom. He listened, then shook his head in wonder.

"More trouble, and you're right there. If you're not the Raven, who is?"

I said, "You really think I'd burn down my own house? I almost died."

He walked to the window and looked out. He knew I was right, but I hadn't answered his question.

"Look, Sergeant," I said, "I have a feeling the Raven won't be bothering us anymore."

"Why do you say that?"

I shrugged. "Just a feeling. Anyway, there's one way to find out. Let's wait and see."

He turned and studied me. "You're a strange kid, David. But I like you. I always did."

I clenched my hand into a fist. After all that had happened, it still felt good.

"You told me the police have a boxing club," I said. "Think I could join?"

He flashed me a tired smile. "I'd like that."

My mom checked me out of the hospital later that day. When I asked where we were going, she was vague. I figured there was a motel room waiting for us.

We turned onto our block and drove slowly past what was left of the house. In the daylight it didn't seem scary at all. It was just a pile of rubble. The only thing left was the chimney. It had outlasted two houses and looked as strong as ever.

We drove farther down the block and parked in front of a shop. The sign said Second Chance.

In front stood Libby and her father.

When we got out of the car, Libby asked my mom, "Did you tell him?"

"Not yet."

Libby turned to me. "Welcome home."

I stared at her.

"There was a vacancy in the apartment next door," she told me. "We're neighbors again."

"It'll be a fresh start," said my mom. "We could both use it."

I noticed my reflection in the shop window. There was a bandage on my arm, and my jaw was swollen.

"I look awful," I said.

Mr. Morales smiled. "A little glue and paint— you'll be as good as new."

* * *

These days, Libby and I walk to school. Some days it's a short trip. Other days it takes longer. Our route goes by the lot where the house used to be. They've put a chain-link fence around it. You can see through the fence. Kids climb over it. It's not the same as a brick wall.

As we walk, we talk about school. We talk about other things too. Sometimes I get mad. I think it's okay.

Recently I've been talking about a different kind of trip. My mom would drive, but in a way I'd be going alone. I would stay for a day or two. Then I'd come back home. It scares me, but I think I can do it.

I'm going to New York.

There was just one story left to tell. It was horrible and terrifying, worthy of the name Poe.

Death would be my masterpiece, death in the manner I had feared most—trapped, unable to escape. I faced my demons, willing myself out of this world and into the next.

You rescued me from the void. You brought me back to life. You chained me to your fury. You watched me explode in flames.

Oh, glorious end!

Now I am going to a place where I might find, at long last, peace.

Good-bye. Thank you.

Ginny, I am coming.

Author's Note

I write historical fiction, and I try to be true to the facts. But when I researched Edgar Allan Poe, it struck me that the facts were incomplete—specifically, the facts about his death.

We know almost nothing about Poe's final days, and what we do know is squalid and sad. He lived in New York, and after his beloved wife, Ginny, died he spent time in Philadelphia and Richmond, trying to raise money for the *Stylus*, a journal of literature and the arts that he dreamed of starting. In October of 1849, Poe found his way to Baltimore, where his writing career had begun and he had spent some of his happiest years. There he was discovered in a tavern, suffering from an unidentified illness, and was taken to a hospital, where he died a few days later. It was reported that before he died, Poe repeatedly called out the name "Reynolds." That's all we know.

Poe deserved a fitting death, not an ignominious one. My goal in writing this book, therefore, wasn't to portray history but to fix it. I took those few facts, built on them, and reimagined his death—not as it was but as it should have been.

What if…

…Poe concocted a final magnificent story that he was determined to live out when he died.

…the plan went terribly wrong and left him trapped in agony between life and death.

…his soul wailed and screamed and grew twisted over time.

...a house sprouted like an evil mushroom—haunted, horrible, worthy of Poe.

...a boy moved there years later and, through his anger, unleashed Poe's spirit.

If you live in Baltimore, don't be surprised when I describe places that don't exist. This is dream Baltimore, other Baltimore, where John Pendleton Kennedy created a monument to his friend, where terror took root in the closet, and where Edgar Allan Poe, at long last, got the death he deserved.

Helen Burrus

Ronald Kidd is the author of thirteen novels for young readers, including the highly acclaimed *Night on Fire* and *Monkey Town: The Summer of the Scopes Trial*. His novels of adventure, comedy, and mystery have received the Children's Choice Award, an Edgar Award nomination, and honors from the American Library Association, the International Reading Association, the Library of Congress, and the New York Public Library. He is a two-time O'Neill playwright who lives in Nashville, Tennessee.